BORVO

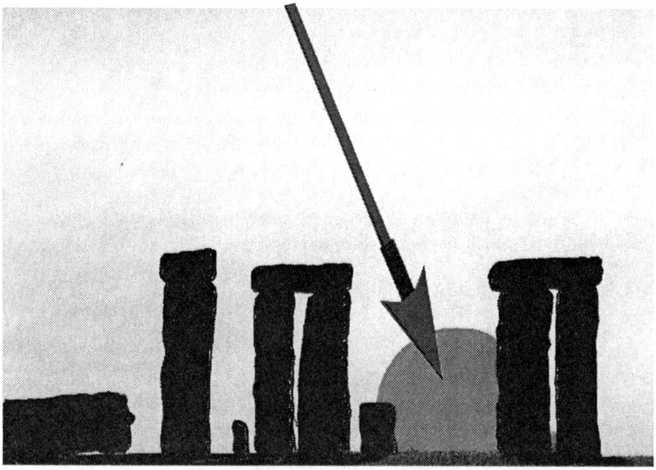

AND THE STONES OF POWER

by

John Margeryson Lord

Order this book online at www.trafford.com/08-0067
or email orders@trafford.com

Most Trafford titles are also available at major online book retailers.

© Copyright 2008 John Margeryson Lord.

All rights reserved. No part of this publication may be reproduced, stored in a retrieval system, or transmitted, in any form or by any means, electronic, mechanical, photocopying, recording, or otherwise, without the written prior permission of the author.

Note for Librarians: A cataloguing record for this book is available from Library and Archives Canada at www.collectionscanada.ca/amicus/index-e.html

Printed in Victoria, BC, Canada.

ISBN: 978-1-4251-6894-0

We at Trafford believe that it is the responsibility of us all, as both individuals and corporations, to make choices that are environmentally and socially sound. You, in turn, are supporting this responsible conduct each time you purchase a Trafford book, or make use of our publishing services. To find out how you are helping, please visit www.trafford.com/responsiblepublishing.html

Our mission is to efficiently provide the world's finest, most comprehensive book publishing service, enabling every author to experience success. To find out how to publish your book, your way, and have it available worldwide, visit us online at www.trafford.com/10510

 www.trafford.com

North America & international
toll-free: 1 888 232 4444 (USA & Canada)
phone: 250 383 6864 ♦ fax: 250 383 6804 ♦ email: info@trafford.com

The United Kingdom & Europe
phone: +44 (0)1865 722 113 ♦ local rate: 0845 230 9601
facsimile: +44 (0)1865 722 868 ♦ email: info.uk@trafford.com

10 9 8 7 6 5 4 3

DEDICATION

This story is dedicated to the creators and the builders of all stone circles, and in particular those who built the greatest and the most famous of them all - Stonehenge.

Their dedication and drive, persistent over several generations, must have been formidable, and we can only gaze upon the results with a mixture of awe and admiration.

A WORD ABOUT STONEHENGE:

I have been of the opinion for some considerable time that its purpose was practical rather that religious or superstitious, and that its orientation was practical rather than based on some natural event or thing such as the position of the sun or that of a particular star. The truth is that we may never know.

INTRODUCTION:

BACKGROUND TO THE STORY

* Timeframe: The events here retailed took place in about 2000 years BC. The great stone circle, that which we now call Stonehenge, was only partially completed, work on the first wooden structure having begun several generations previously and the construction work of mounting the great Sarson uprights was now underway. Britain was mostly heavily forested and travel on foot over large distances was difficult, time consuming and could be dangerous. Tracks were few and mostly hard to follow but were used by occasional traders, and carriers of news, the latter being the Story Singers of these events. The people of the time were as intelligent and had the same emotional drives and intellectual ambitions as modern day humans, their limitations stemmed from living in the timeframe of the stone-age and at the beginning of bronze-age technology.

* The Story Singers: These are a pure invention, but something of this kind must have been in operation to account for the stone circles springing up from the northernmost of the Scottish islands to the South coast of England.

* Language: A common language probably did not then exist, clans would have their own informal versions, but with the advent of the Story Singers and the rapid increase in trade an embryonic general means of communication must have begun to thrive. Stonehenge could not have been built without it.

* The North and South Realms of Kingdoms: These are also an invention intended to convey the kind of loose structure that may have been developing naturally as interaction became more common.

* Places: The stone circles referred to in the story are real and are located as follows -
Chapter 5 - Castlerigg Circle near Keswick in the Lake District.
Chapter 11 - The Bull Ring at Dove Holes in Derbyshire
Chapter 12 - The Fort - Castle Naze on Combs Edge in Derbyshire
Chapter 15 - Arbor Low in Derbyshire
Chapter 19 & onwards - Stonehenge

* Route: The routes travelled (as far as they are known) are shown on the map Appendix A.

JOHN MARGERYSON LORD

CONTENTS

Dedication iii
A Word About Stonehenge: Iii
Background To The Story..Iv

Death of A Chief.. 1
Tallon Is Laid In His Grave 5
The Story Singers... 11
It Begins..23
The Stones Challenged...31
Born To Rule 41
Committed..49
Return..59
Banished..63
Avilla..71
Bork Marches South 79
The Fort...85
Thief...87
Revenge 93
Herik..101
Warnings and Preparations for War......................................109
Winter Quarters..115
Stopped..123

Arrival 131
The Great Stone Circle - Under Construction 141
The Great Stone Circle (1) 143
The Great Stone Circle (2) 153
Responsibility 163
News 171
Preparations 181
Bork Continues His March South 189
Bork Arrives 195
Night-time 201
Before The Storm 205
Pre - Dawn 207
Dawn 217
Afterwards 225

Appendix A Route Map 229
Appendix B Route and Timetable 230
Appendix C Main Characters 232

CHAPTER 1

❧ DEATH OF A CHIEF ❧

*T*he air was thick and heavy. Huge dense black clouds hung still over the cluster of small dwellings. Zapallor the soothsayer had predicted a storm and the earth seemed to be paused - waiting for it, holding its breath.

Avilla began to be afraid. He felt the acid taste of it well into his throat. Facing him stood Tallon, his elder brother and clan chief, his face contorted with rage, his dark eyes black with hate. Tallon's fury had been brewing for several days and was now about to boil over. Dread paralysed Avilla as he realised that this time Tallon's anger had him in its grip and there were not any words in the world to sooth him.

Smaller than Avilla, Tallon was a thoroughbred fighter with the strength of any two men. What was worse Avilla was unarmed and he saw that Tallon gripped a hunting dagger in each fist their metal glinting in a thin shaft of sunlight as it slanted through a small gap in the dark clouds. The chief also had the protection of stout leather body armour. Avilla felt naked as he faced this growling spitting animal of a man now clearly bent on killing him.

Then, before Avilla had any chance to defend himself Tallon with a howl of fury launched himself across the intervening gap stabbing with all the force he could command.

Taken by surprise, Avilla tried to screw himself away but felt the shock of pain as the dagger in Talon's right hand entered his chest and saw his blood staining his clothing. The weapon's point struck his rib and its point broke away lodged in the bone. In spite of the searing pain Avilla tried with all his remaining strength to avoid the thrust of Tallon's second weapon but it sliced through his right thigh leaving a deep gash and causing Avilla to fall forward and collapse on top of the smaller Tallon.

By now a small crowd had gathered and stood silently watching events with apprehension, not daring to support either party for fear of the winner's wrath, for it was now plain that only one of the combatants would survive.

The world was suddenly shattered by a searing flash of lightning temporarily blinding the fighters and the watchers.

The two bodies fell in a tangle of limbs and as the air was torn by a crash of thunder they wrestled on the dusty earth, each striving to find an advantage over the other.

Avilla was loosing blood and felt his strength ebbing away, but he suddenly found in the melee that he was looking at Tallon's only vulnerable flesh, Tallon's neck was but inches from his face. Gathering all his remaining strength he bit hard into Tallon's throat and was rewarded with a strangled scream as his teeth severed his opponent's main artery and his life's blood sprayed out of the wound in great pulsing jets. At which point Avilla passed out.

The watching crowd gave a long low groan at the sight of the chief's blood mingled with that of Avilla. Such a thing had never happened before. Many hid their faces and moved quickly away for no one knew what might happen next.

The storm was fading as Avilla came to and found that he was lying on his back, his wounds being dressed by two of the clan's women healers. On the ground beside him was the grey lifeless body of Tallon, and Avilla's first coherent thought was that the clan now had no leader. His second thought was for Tallon's woman Chine and their young son Bork.

Almost immediately that Avilla opened his eyes the women were thrust aside by Tallon's two bodyguard-henchmen who stood over Avilla with raised spears poised to avenge their chief's death, but before they could deliver a killing thrust several of the the watching crowd intervened to stop them with a great shout of `No', and then they in their turn were pushed away, leaving the healers to finish their work.

The sight of his father's dead body lying still splashed in blood was young Bork's earliest memory, and it stayed with him all his life. It was to affect him and thus the tribe and even the whole of the then known world in the months to come. As he grew older the need to avenge his father's death took hold of him and became his life's prime purpose, but as yet, in his youth, he had neither the resources nor the ability to deal with Avilla -

- that person's fate would have to wait - but Bork was certain the opportunity would come. He would ensure that it did.

The storm gradually retreated to a distant rumble and the clouds withdrew allowing pale sunlight to bathe the terrible scene, a scene that all who witnessed it would never forget.

Avilla had the bodyguard-henchmen gently carry Tallon's body to his and Chine's dwelling where it was laid out on his tressle bed.

Darkness slowly invaded the deserted scene, which was now given over to the creatures of the night.

Most slept little or not at all, their minds full of the recent shattering event.

Avilla tried not to think as pain took him over in great waves. He thought that he had little chance of survival.

CHAPTER 2

✢ **TALLON IS LAID IN HIS GRAVE** ✣

*L*ife in the North was harsh, brutal, and often very short. There was only one rule over-riding all others - survival. To do so one had to keep it at the front of one's mind every waking moment. At thirty-five one was considered to be old, and death at childbirth was more common than life.

Priority was given at all times by survivors to just two paramount needs - food and shelter - all other activities being considered to be pure indulgence only permitted in rare times of plenty.

Women were considered to be more important to the clan than men, since they were vital to replace the losses of clan members.

However, the loss of the clan leader was very serious, and a grave set-back to the group. Concern for the clan's survival ran high especially as his son Bork was still too young and inexperienced for the heavy task.

For all his fearful faults and prejudices Tallon, whose name meant Eagle, had been a strong and courageous fighter. In the many battles with would be attackers he had never been defeated and had won many of his own initiated fights.

The clan had depended on him - and now he had gone.

Clearly something had to be done about the leadership; but before anything could be decided Tallon's body had to be dealt with honour and ceremony. So for the moment the corrosive friction between the brothers Tallon and Avilla and their supporters was set aside as Tallon's body was prepared for burial and his favourite possessions collected for internment with him.

Tallon's bodyguard-henchmen Terck and Sollin were by popular consent given the honour of preparing a grave in the nearby mound of stones where his ancestors already lay.

And just two days after the fateful fight which ended his life Tallon's grave was ready and it was time. The morning broke sunny and bright but instead of the usual noise of chatter and domestic activities a sombre quiet held the living space.

Aware of the momentous crisis gripping the future and conscious of the traditions of the present, the people stood or sat waiting silently in small family groups outside the scattered dwellings.

Several low homes lay loosely arranged round a central open-air hearth, each was made of a circle of stones supporting a roof of cut branches the whole thing being covered with a layer of sods. The finished quality of each of these living quarters reflected the skill of its owner. Some were neatly built even decorated, others exhibited the bare minimum of creative skill. This clan group of dwellings lay near the middle of a wide grassy space that had been laboriously cut from the surrounding forest.

The place being sited atop a large natural hill surrounded by a deep man made ditch and earth mound. A crude wooden fence was mounted on top of the mound as a first defence against would be intruders and marauding animals.

This had been the home of Tallon's clan for at least three generations and would be for many more. The people liked it and were successful - they survived.

On this day the summer sun climbed higher in the clear blue sky, and slowly, singly and in groups all the people from babes to ancients began to arrive before the burial place.

They did not talk.

When all were assembled, Tallon's body now resplendent in his battle refinery was carried by his bodyguard-henchmen in complete silence to the ancestral mound and was placed with great care in the hollow prepared for it. His two metal daggers the point of one missing still painfully lodged in Avilla's rib, his bow, two short fighting spears and one long hunting spear, and his favourite drinking bowl were then placed tenderly beside him and a lid of stones levered into place.

As his son Bork was still too young to take the responsibility it fell to Avilla to say the praises of the dead.

Still weak from his wounds and loss of blood, leaning with his whole weight on a stick, heavily drugged to dull the pain, his face ashen, it took all his available strength to stand unaided. He shook with physical hurt and emotion.

The group stood still each concerned face reflecting the dreadful seriousness of the occasion.

Slowly Avilla turned to the grave and addressed the dead chief in a low voice that trembled and hesitated but which could be heard by all present in the morning quiet.

'I...., I killed you my brother........,' he managed and paused. Then more strongly, `and yet I loved you......., I loved you as our gifted leader....., as a friend....., and above all as my kin................... Your death has given me, your son, your wife, and the whole clan much pain.'

'From the day you took over from your ailing father you have governed us well, and for this we give you our thanks, and we have survived............... But now until your good son Bork is grown enough to take your place we will have no one of your courage and fighting spirit to lead us and you will be greatly missed.'

'For these things I honour and salute you my brother.'

With this said, Avilla then painfully turned to face the people and spoke directly to Bork whose expression showed the emotion he was feeling, determined as he was to be the man his father would acknowledge.

'You, his son, will in time take your father's place at the head of the clan and I am certain you will lead us well for I see you already show the signs of his character which we will need if we are to continue.

'You must know that I did not pick this fight that took his life, your father did. I hope that one day you will come to understand this and to forgive my awful deed. In the meantime you have my trust and full support.'

Then raising his face to the sky Avilla announced loudly and in a clear voice -

'Long live Tallon's, now Bork's clan.'

He then bowed his head towards Bork and was silent.

The ceremony was at an end.

Bork stood still ashen faced not daring to trust himself to speak.

Suddenly the eerie silence which followed was shattered as a pair of crows descended onto the burial mound and began to fight fiercely and noisily. Later Zapallor the soothsayer was asked, and with great reluctance, gave her opinion as to what this meant.

Alone with Bork and Avilla, white faced and solemn she pronounced -

`The black crows were sent by Tallon who is not yet at rest with the ancestors and is telling us that the fight that killed him will not cease whilst Bork and Avilla both live.'

Bork and Avilla stared coldly at each other, but only Bork knew that her words were the truth.

Tragically for the clan's future, Bork's pain did not end with his father's burial nor with Avilla's fine speech. Instead it twisted the hurt in his heart and he determined to avenge his father's death by seeing Avilla killed. The animosity that caused the hatred that Tallon had for Avilla had its source in a fundamental difference in how the clan should be ruled. It was a sore that had brought pain to the relationship between the brothers and had found its final outlet in the fight that ended Tallon's life.

This same hatred was now invested in Bork.

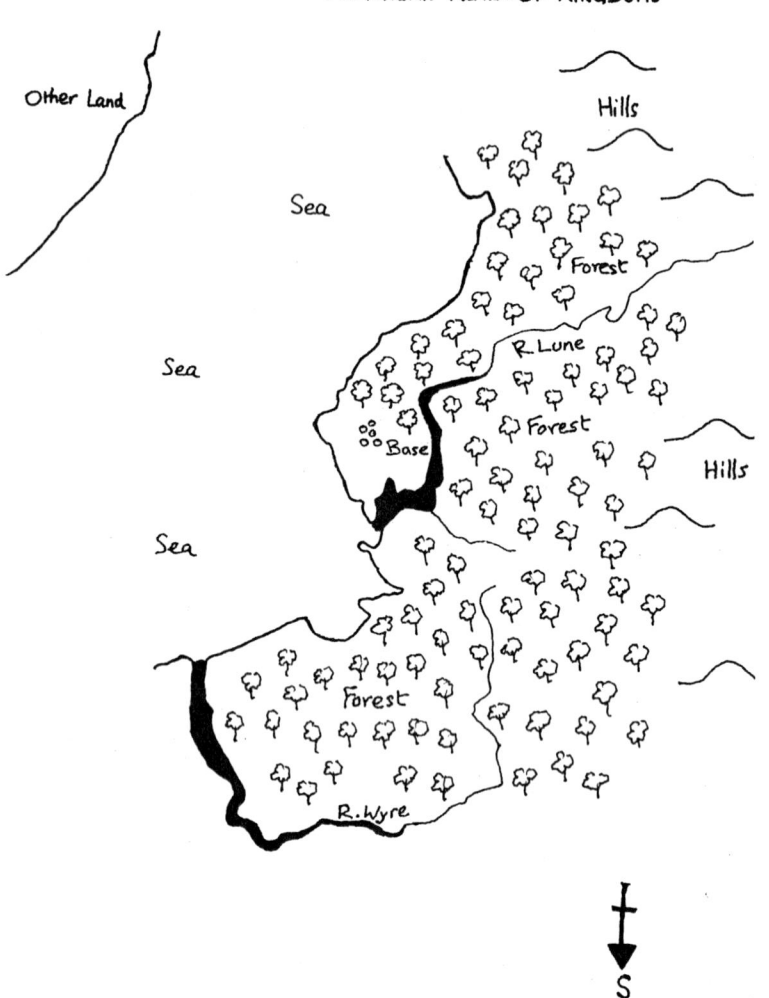

AREA KNOWN TO BORK'S CLAN

CHAPTER 3

༒ **THE STORY SINGERS** ༒

*A*villa was used to living in the shadow of his older brother, but as he grew to manhood it became ever more irksome.

Tallon was a fighting man whose determination for the clan to survive rested on his eliminating by means of force any one or anything that attempted to stand in his way.

A shortage of food was solved by raiding a neighbouring clan, taking all he needed and leaving the rest, usually the elderly and the helpless to starve. In this he had proved extremely successful and was recognised by most of the other local clans as their Lord.

He had in fact become the effective ruler of what was becoming known as the Northern Realm of Kingdoms.

There was another group of clans often sung about by the story singers. They lived mostly well to the south of Bork's clan and were known by the collective name of the Southern Realm of Kingdoms. In both realms each clan as it grew was completely autonomous ruled over by a clan member or chief and therefore they became thought of as small independent kingdoms

Not only were these two realms separated by geography and sheer distance, but their purposes and manner of living were fundamentally different. The clans of the south had begun to forego fighting each other in favour of a loose cooperation. This brand new and alternative way of life was assisted by a somewhat less harsh climate, and importantly a significantly more fertile environment.

Much to Tallon's disdain, Avilla weary of battles and useless deaths had come to believe that the ways of the south were superior and should be adopted.

At first Tallon tolerated his younger brother's views putting them down to youthful naivety, but as Avilla grew to manhood, some members of the clan started to listen to his arguments and Tallon as chief saw this as a challenge to his authority and threatened Avilla with dismissal from the clan if he persisted.

This difference between the two became a sore and then an open wound in their relationship, which Tallon was unable to heal.

Then Terck, one of Tallon's bodyguard-henchmen, reported to the chief that Avilla had been trying to persuade the younger men of the clan not to fight other clans but to seek their cooperation in such ways as joining in the hunting parties or sharing scarce resources.

At this Tallon knew his authority was at risk and sought Avilla out to face him. He knew that there could only ever be one chief and this had to be himself.

The argument, Tallon thought should take place in view of the rest of the clan or at least those to whom it might be of interest. This was no private argument - it affected the whole clan. And so it was arranged. Tallon with his two bodyguard-henchmen accosted Avilla hoping to surprise him without a prepared defence.

There was a storm brewing.

Avilla saw the serious faces of the three and guessed their purpose. His heart sank.

This argument was not to his liking, he was not prepared.

To begin with Tallon kept his temper under control.

'I have been advised that you have been trying to persuade our fighters to disobey me, ' he began. 'You must cease to discuss your unacceptable views with others,' he stated, 'they are wicked and wrong and if adopted will weaken the clan. These sun worshippers you believe in are simply misguided fools who will come to a bad end.'

It was an order and he expected to be obeyed without question.

Avilla tried to explain.

'But if you would just listen - it seems to work and.........'

Tallon interrupted him.

'Did you hear me? How dare you challenge my authority. I am chief here and I will not tolerate your disobedience.'

But now, in the face of such a refusal to listen, a convinced Avilla refused to back down.

'You are wrong to dismiss what may be a better way of life,' he said angrily. He too believed that he knew what was best for the clan. 'You and your wars are out of date, you should wake up and embrace the new manner of living.'

At this Tallon whose temper was always short and who was already at the limits of his self control, gave in completely to his anger,

He saw this simply as a direct challenge to himself as chief made doubly intolerable by being by this idiot of a younger brother. His fury engulfed him and seizing his daggers he flew at Avilla clearly intending to make an example of him and his hated views. If necessary he would kill him, these ideas had to be eliminated. Thus began that fatal fight between the brothers which ended in Tallon's death.

****

Bork had much in common with his father and as the lad grew it became clear that as far as clan leadership was concerned there would be little change. Father and son were even built on similar lines, both being short and stocky but immensely strong. Bork had even inherited his father's slightly malformed leg which caused it to be somewhat shorter than the other. This gave Bork a characteristic rolling motion when walking, exaggerated noticeably when he ran. Although he was embarrassed by this it in no way hindered his effectiveness as a fighting man. Added to this was his father's stubbornness and his short temper.

He had listened often to his father's views and had determined to continue to uphold the old ancestral ways. This would eventually bring him, into conflict with Avilla.

****

It was seven days after the fight that ended Tallon's life and rule when two children who had been out foraging along one of the many forest trails returned to announce that the story singers were on their way to visit the clan.

The story singers were small groups of two or three, seldom more, adults who tramped the ancient paths that criss-crossed through forests and over hills throughout the then known land. Unlike the clans they lived in tiny secretive groups hidden well away from the main forest trails. Always on the move, they carried knowledge and stories of other people and places which they committed to song which they then re-told in exchange for food, drink and accommodation. As an essential source of news they always travelled safely, were never molested and were always made welcome on arrival. They and the occasional travelling trader were the only links between the peoples of the known world, and as such their rare visits were occasions for great excitement and festivities.

So Avilla, who had temporarily assumed the position of clan chief until Bork had proved himself capable of the task, gave instructions to make the story singers welcome, and the people happily responded. Food and drinks were prepared and a good fire lit as a sign of good will.

A cheer went up as the two male singers emerged from the trees, but before they were fed and despite everyone wanting to talk to them at the same time with questions flying from all sides, -

'What are you called?'

'Where have you come from?'

'Have you seen any game, if so where?'

'Are you going to sing for us?'

'Do you have women?'

Avilla took them aside and sat down with them, Tallon's bodyguard-henchmen and Bork being the only others present.

'Let me introduce Terck and Sollin, Tallon's and now Bork's bodyguard-henchmen, and also our future leader, Tallon's son, Bork,' Avilla began.

The two bowed to Bork and tallest singer replied graciously.

'We know Terck and Sollin as experienced hunters, your reputations precede you. And we are pleased to meet you Bork, son of Tallon. I am Yorg and this is Pladge.

And you good Avilla we have met before, but where is Tallon himself, is he sick?'

'No, with sadness I have to tell you that Tallon is now with his ancestors.'

Avilla's bald statement was received in shocked silence by the singers. They said nothing and waited. Clearly there was a story here which they must turn into song and commit to memory.

Then slowly, leaving nothing unsaid, Avilla told of the fight just as it was.

But as he listened Bork felt his anger rise.

'My father was murdered.' he said through clenched teeth.

This was greeted in silence as they waited respectfully for Bork to regain some composure.

Yorg then spoke. 'We thank you for your sad news, which was well told. We know how painful this must be. Your story will be sung, and such was Tallon's reputation that you may experience challenges to your position as the Northern Realm's strongest clan. You must be on your guard and ready.'

'Now see what danger you have put us in,' Bork ground out pointing a trembling finger at Avilla.

To which Avilla made no reply, but insisted that the singers join the rest of the people and sing the latest stories

\- to which they gratefully agreed and followed Avilla to the welcoming fire, to be presented with food and drink.

****

The sun was sinking over the forest where the night animal sounds were beginning to replace those of the day. And having satisfied their hunger the singers sat and waited for silence as they faced eager faces. Everyone was there, even the smallest. This was an occasion not to be missed. Even the poorly were gently carried out and given front seats.

As the noise abated the singers began, each taking their turn to sing a verse telling tales of grand and small events that had taken place amongst the northern tribes which they had recently visited.

There was news of new lives beginning, of old lives ending, of a great catch of deer, of a pure white stag, and of an unresolved dispute between two women of one of the smaller clans over a man who wanted nothing to do with either of them. This last tale made everyone laugh.

Suddenly the tone of the songs changed and the atmosphere became charged with tension. The singers now had every ear. This was serious.

The singers took a drink, settled themselves more comfortably, and facing the circle of eager faces prepared to render their last news song of the day.

Bork, anxious not to miss a single word moved closer.

In the quiet they began.

First singer:
'We have a tale to tell of wondrous things,
Of strange doings not explained.

Never before as we travel the north,
Have our eyes been shown what the earth brought forth.'

Both:
'Stones, stones,
Stones of magic.'

Second singer:
'From the very ground,
Great heavy stones have been found.
These were then stood high on end,
As if to the sky a message send.'

Both:
'Stones, stones,
A ring of stones.'

First singer:
'Of mystery more we will sing,
These stones were mounted in a ring.
Their purpose to us unknown,
No rule or spell to us was shown.'

Both:
'Stones, stones,
Mysterious stones.'

Second singer:
'As we watched a meet begun,
The people gathered to watch the sun.

They took some message unannounced,
And future action was pronounced.'

Both:
'Stones, stones,
Stones of power.'

First singer:
'More of this we cannot tell,
The story must for lack of knowing finish here,
Of secrets hidden from our ear,
We will not let our minds to dwell.'

Both:
'Stones, stones,
What do you stand for?'

After which the only sound was the crackling of the fires glowing embers, for none present could divine the song's meaning. Later they would ask Zapallor if she could shed any light on what the singers had witnessed.

The singers then sang a nonsense rhyme for the children which everyone enjoyed and the evening ended on a lighter note.

But amongst the older members of the clan discussions began which lasted well into the night. Never before had such a strange story been told but somehow its importance had been recognised. Life would not be he same again. Centuaries of the old ways were about to be challenged. It would in some way affect every single living person.

However, as yet the meaning was a mystery.

****

A couple of days later the singers said their farewells and thanked Avilla and the clan for their hospitality and set off to continue their journey south. They had only gone a short distance when they were halted by the animated figure of Bork standing in their way waving them to stop. They stopped and waited.

'Why did you come here upsetting the people with these mad tales of great rings of stone. Many are now afraid and you are the cause. The damage is serious. It was news only suitable for a chief.' Here Bork alluded to himself. 'But to scare the rest was irresponsible. Should this occur again you will cease to be welcome.'

At this Yorg pointed to a nearby log and calmly suggested they sat, and both singers did so - Bork defiantly remained standing his face clouded with anger.

'We hold you and your views in deep respect,' Yorg began, 'and if you insist we will reserve any serious information for you alone, should you require it. But please consider what might happen if on a visit to another clan your men came suddenly upon one of these rings of stones. What do you imagine they would think or do?'

He paused to let this sink in.

'And please remember our reputation and our very lives rest on telling about all we see and know. If we didn't could you lay any value to our words?'

Bork stood and was silent, an emotional storm raging within him, the anguish of it showing on his face. Then with a visible struggle he drew himself together.

'You will always be welcome here as it was with my father so with me.'

This said Bork turned and walked away his head bowed in deep thought.

This had been his first real lesson as future clan leader, he was glad there were no witnesses and hoped the singers would not relate that which had just taken place.

They did not.

CHAPTER 4

⸗ IT BEGINS ⸗

The wounds sustained by Avilla in his fight with Tallon kept him from taking part in hunting and foraging trips for some time.

Bork's bodyguard-henchmen took it upon themselves to take their new master in hand and teach him all they could about the job of providing for the clan. They planned to pass on all those skills that Tallon had shown them. In this they were often away for long periods, and returned too exhausted to join the clan's evening get-togethers round the fire. Thus it was that they lost touch with clan gossip. When he did catch up Bork was severely shaken by what he learned.

One of the several women who tended Avilla's wounds which were washed and dressed every day, was Chine - Tallon's woman and Bork's mother.

Much younger than Tallon, she was nearer Avilla's age and was still agile and very attractive. She had since Tallon's death been pestered by several would-be suitors all of whom she had gently but sternly turned away.

Avilla, tall, lean but with a powerful muscle structure was not unpleasing to the opposite sex, and Chine had plenty of time close to Avilla to appreciate his physical qualities.

Her life with Tallon had not been easy, his foul temper was never far below the surface and life with him could be frightening and sometimes extremely painful.

She had learned the hard way how to handle her volatile man. Her situation eased a little when Bork was born - as the birth of a boy child and future clan chief was an honour which gave rise to lengthy celebrations, and accorded her a senior place in the clan's hierarchy.

Avilla, attracted to Chine, did his best to keep his relationship with her under control, that is simply as patient and nurse. However he grew to know the tender aspect of her nature, and found that she had strong opinions about most important matters and he learned to trust her word and to value her judgement. He was in fact falling deeply in love.

For her part Chine when dealing with the wound on Avilla's thigh could not avoid noticing his manhood respond to the soothing caress of her hands. She listened with interest to Avilla's dreams of a more peaceful way of life and found that they resonated favourably with her gentle nature. She was in fact also falling in love.

They both knew the risks involved should Bork ever suspect their mutual attraction and did all they could to hide it. They avoided each other as much as was possible in their tiny community, but some interaction was inevitable and their mutual consideration became a matter of clan gossip. It was then just a matter of time before they declared their feelings towards each other and just a little more time before they expressed this physically.

****

Meanwhile Bork was growing up fast. He even astounded all present with his courage at his very first hunt. The event became quite famous and was later put into song by the story singers.

A youth who had been exploring in the nearby forest came dashing excitedly in to tell of a fine stag wandering on its own just a short distance into the trees. He was instantly brought before Bork and the bodyguard-henchmen and given the job of guide. A stag represented good meat for several days, large antlers to make tough strong tools, and a good sized hide had many uses - a valuable prize in fact.

So a hunting party of six men headed by Bork and armed with hunting spears set off to follow the guide into the trees and was soon lost from view. It was autumn and the trees were dripping with moisture from the early morning mists which were just lifting. Despite moving with great care, they kept up a good pace with Bork leading the hunters with his strange rolling gait caused by his short right leg. Eventually their guide slowed to a careful walk and signalled with his finger to his lip for quiet. Suddenly he stopped, checked the wind direction and then as silently as possible led them round until they faced into the slight breeze that barely stirred the leaves. Peering through the trees he pointed straight ahead, and through the branches they saw standing stock still, head raised fully alert was a majestic adult stag. It carried its antlers high showing by the number of points that it was at least eight years of age, a fully grown and mature beast.

As there were no hinds with him the stag was an old bachelor and alone.

The party hefted their spears and prepared to charge but before they could there was a deep snorting grunt from the nearby undergrowth and the shape of an enormous boar hurled itself full tilt at the stag, with the same intention as the party.

Then several things happened in rapid succession. The stag jumped and leaped away quickly vanishing amongst the trees. The boar, head down charged after it. Bork swore and threw himself after the boar.

Taken by surprise the rest of the hunters started to run after Bork. Although not in view the route taken by Bork and the animals was easy to follow. So intent were they that they nearly ran into Bork who was peering into the mouth of a natural cave half hidden by the undergrowth.

Bork told them that the stag had escaped but the boar had taken refuge in the cave.

He then astounded the little group by announcing that he would go in and get the boar.

Now fighting a boar in the open with several men armed with hunting spears was hazard enough, but one man faced with a cornered animal fighting for its life was suicide, and the men tried hard to dissuade Bork.

But a stubborn, brave, and determined Bork hefted his spear and bending low crept slowly into the cave. The watchers held their breath. Then their ears were assailed by the frightful noise of the boar's shrieks of pain mingled with Bork's bellowed curses, and they stepped back expecting the worse.

Then came a terrible silence.

Out of the cave stumbled a bent figure covered in blood and carrying the shaft of a broken spear.

'I killed it,' whispered Bork and promptly collapsed.

The party were horrified at seeing the deep gouges in Bork's flesh, and wondered how he could still be alive. The pessimists expected him to die before they got him back.

Stretchers of branches were made for both man and beast and they were carried somewhat gingerly back with Bork still showing some life by cursing every bump and jostle. He even tried to persuade the hunters to go back with him for the stag. On arrival people immediately gathered round to gazed with awe and admiration at the pair.

Bork barely survived but had begun to establish his image as an invincible fighter.

Early the next day those same hunters set out to find the stag before the wolves did Bork even tried to order them to take him with them, an order that was universally ignored.

They found and killed the animal, their return with their booty being celebrated much to Bork's obvious annoyance.

Bork did everything possible to shorten his convalescence, practicing at all hours with daggers and spear. He was so engrossed in this and another problem that was starting to bedevil his every waking moment that he missed that which Avilla and Chine were trying to hide.

The issue that was beginning to take over Bork's mind was the picture that the story singers had conjured up for him - of that clan to the north building their ring of stones. The purpose of such a structure he could not even begin to guess at. Nor could he fathom why that clan had put such a huge amount of effort into doing such a thing. But of one thing he was utterly convinced - the ring's purpose was evil and all it stood for was against his very nature. He became convinced that the stone circle had to be destroyed and soon before its influence was allowed to spread.

When consulted Zapallor was non-committal about the stones saying that the only influence they possessed was that which was in the minds of those who chose to put it there, the stones themselves being harmless. This sound advice was rejected by Bork who had already decided to take action against them.

It was no surprise to Bork that Avilla was dubious about any attempt to attack the clan and destroy the circle. But he would order Avilla to join the expedition to demonstrate to him where the real power lay.

And so it was that having fully recovered Bork called the clan together to announce his intention to conduct a raid on the circle building clan, and to identify those men he would take with him. As winter with its own survival problems was now upon them, the expedition would take place as soon as the snow had melted in the spring.

He had expected the clan to be enthusiastic as to his plan and was considerably angered by their obvious non-committal shrug of the shoulders, This was not a normal raid for provisions and no one knew what to expect. Perhaps the stones really did have some terrible magical power.

This was the unknown and they were very wary of the unknown.

Very conscious of the lack of support for his plan, Bork decided to conduct a surprise raid on a clan they had heard about from the story singers. This small group lived just across the river to the north and Bork hoped to be able to persuade some of the more able men to join him in his attack on the stone circle encampment.

The days were growing longer and warmer, buds were beginning to show the green of young leaves. Except on the very high ground the snow had vanished.

Bork and his bodyguard-henchmen rounded up his troop, appraised them of his intentions, and told them to be ready to march at dawn in two days.

A key part of the plan was to raid a small group known to reside en route in order to collect provisions for the main march north and the unknown.

A horrified Avilla found that his influence over events was waning as Bork's position and stature was now being recognised, and not wishing to compromise Chine he collected his weapons and reported with the rest.

Thus a small troop of hardened fighter-hunters set out with Bork at its head. Conditions were favourable and after a single day's march they crossed the river by way of an ancient bridge of felled trees, and arrived within striking distance of Bork's intended initial target.

It was easy for the scouts to identify when they were close - paths appeared and became numerous and well used. Trees showed where branches had been lopped for building purposes and for fuel. At this point Bork halted the troop, and as his father had taught him he sent Terck ahead to announce his intention to attack unless the clan decided to surrender.

Terck was not gone long and immediately reported to Bork.

`Their chief wants to confer with you. He said that if you agree he will meet with you out here, he will be alone and unarmed.'

Without consulting Avilla Bork agreed, and Terck soon returned from his second visit to the clan accompanied by a tall, imposing youthful warrior.

'He does not carry a weapon,' Terck announced. 'This is the clan chief.'

Bork bowed, introduced himself and nodding for the newcomer to follow him set off into the trees so that their conversation could not be overheard.

They were not gone long, and on returning it was plain that both were happy with the outcome.

To the surprise of the would-be raiders the clan offered no resistance. Instead they were made welcome. They told Bork that they too had had a visit from the story singers, and had learned about the stone circle building group, and like Bork they feared it and a few even offered to join Bork's small army to which Bork readily agreed.

This was indeed good news for Bork and after a day's rest the enhanced small army set off, again heading north, to find and destroy the circle builders.

Avilla was in despair but held his tongue. He felt ever more strongly that this was a wrong for which they might all pay a terrible price in human suffering. It seemed to him that they were playing with forces much stronger than themselves whilst being ignorant as to what dreadful power they might unleash. He knew that it would be impossible to try to dissuade Bork from this plan in which all their lives might be at risk. He hid his despair, again held his tongue, and wished he had Chine's sensible council to guide him.

CHAPTER 5

⇜ **THE STONES CHALLENGED** ⇝

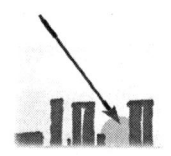

So Bork's small enhanced army made preparations to march farther north. Each man was apprehensive as to what they would find and what would be the ultimate outcome of this unique confrontation. But rested now and loaded with provisions they set off to face the unknown. No-one from either clan had ventured this far north before and they had some difficulty finding the route taken by the story singers. Often a way had to be cut through dense groups of trees clogged by thick undergrowth. Bork was conscious of the toll this was taking of the men as day by day they struggled forward. Their daily progress grew less and the time spent recovering grew longer. Doubts were being muttered, mostly out of Bork's hearing. They found themselves facing new dangers, rivers and high mountains had to be negotiated and this demanded leadership of the highest order and to Avilla's surprise Bork handled each situation like a veteran of more mature years. His men began to respect and trust him.

Then after four long day's struggle Bork's forward scout returned to report that they were within an hour's march of their goal, and trembling with fear he told of seeing a ring of monstrous upright stones. On Bork's questioning he also said that there appeared to be no-one about, and still shaking he described the area as a broad open space carved out of the trees on a slight slope and visible from some distance away, it would be impossible to reach the stones without exposing oneself to an enemy hiding nearby. The whole place was overlooked by towering mountains which reared up and vanished into the clouds. He suspected that their presence was known and an ambush awaited them. There was, he added, no sign of any dwellings.

Bork sat with his bodyguard-henchmen and Avilla to review their position.

This was a new situation and they had no precedent to go by. Unsurprisingly Avilla was for sending an envoy forward to negotiate.

'We are here to destroy this superstition, there will be no negotiation,' growled a furious Bork.

Avilla stayed silent.

'The men are tired and in need of rest,' Terck pointed out.

In the end Bork decided to attack the stones directly at dawn the next day, and appointed an overnight watch with everyone taking a session in turn.

****

Dawn broke fine and even the early sun was warm. A bad sign, Bork was hoping for the cover of an early mist. He had ordered silence and there was little noise as the small troop fed and prepared for the fray.

Ready at last, with Bork at its head the small army crept forward through the trees, their progress being covered by the noise if the wind in the leaves and the chorus of the early bird songs which seemed to surround them.

Apprehension showed on the face of every man.

Forward progress was slow, but on they crept, taking full advantage of every bit of cover.

Suddenly Bork stopped and held up his hand, no one moved. They knew that he had reached the edge of the clearing in the centre of which loomed the circle of upright stones.

Only Bork showed a lack of fear, his determination paramount.

Turning to his troop he reported seeing no one about and ordered them to follow him into the clearing.

Bork then marched boldly out to stand facing the imposing circle of stones.

His men followed apprehensively and stopped in a half circle behind him. They stood trembling in awe. None had seen anything like this before, superstition and fright gripped each man, and each was desperately trying to overcome a terrible desire to turn and run, but fear of Bork's wrath and their personal pride prevented them.

There was an eerie silence into which, with a shout a figure armed with a spear appeared seemingly out of nowhere. He stood in front of the stones and confronted the army aggressively brandishing his weapon, his face suffused with rage.

And there he stood, a solitary and lonely challenger, clearly prepared to confront Bork and his men.

No one moved.

All were silent.

Then to everyone's surprise Bork walked forward and stood just a few short paces in front of the defender.

'Surrender or die,' he shouted.

'If I die so do you,' the other replied.

'I have no need of these to crush you.' Bork said and threw his dagger and spear to the ground.

He's lost his mind thought Avilla.

But immediately the defender discarded his own tools of war, and advanced a few steps towards Bork.

Bork then threw himself at the man and they grasped each other in close combat.

The fight lasted just a few minutes as it became clear that they were about equally matched and the conflict was halted by the armed intervention of Bork's bodyguard-henchmen.

The pair stood bloodily and stared at each other with mutual respect.

Suddenly Bork laughed and held out his hand to the other who after hesitating grasped it grinning.

'Name yourself,' demanded Bork.

'I am Drng which here means oak tree.'

'And I am Bork son of Tallon.'

'I have heard of you Bork son of Tallon from the story singers and your father's fame is known to me also. Welcome to this place. I am sorry for the unwelcoming reception.'

'Then Drng you must know that we are here on a dread purpose. We aim to destroy this foul monument to superstition.' Bork's expression was grim as he waved his hand at the circle of stones.

The reply was a surprise.

'Then do your worst,' said Drng, 'and let any misfortune which may follow be on your own head.'

At this there was a murmur of dissent from Bork's men.

'Take no notice,' said Bork addressing them directly, 'it's all superstition - we will do what we came here to do.'

He then directed several of his men, and with them advanced to the nearest stone where together they put their shoulders to it.

A ragged cheer went up as the stone wobbled a little and then fell on to its side.

Their satisfaction was however short lived. The lying stone was balanced such that the bulk of its weight lay at its base and whilst they stood and watched the stone fell back into the hole it had just vacated and stood up again on its end without any help.

An awe struck group stood silent.

This was powerful magic. Even Bork was visibly shaken.

Avilla was the first to find his tongue, and with his face contorted in anger he shouted at Bork. 'You simple minded idiot, you have no knowledge of what you may have done, you will bring disaster down on all of us with your stupid warring.'

Even Bork stood trembling at this.

And the power the stones now held would have commanded them but for a strange and humorous incident which followed.

A crashing noise and a shouting shattered the silence as a man of enormous girth hurled himself from the trees. Following hard on his heels was a fully grown wolf with teeth bared. The figure was unable to stop and crashed headlong into another of the stones. Such was his weight and momentum that the stone fell immediately - and this time it stayed down.

Before the wolf reached the newcomer who was now lying on the grass defenceless, a whistle sounded and to the surprise of Bork and his men the wolf trotted over to Drng and sat quietly at his feet. This gave rise to much hilarity.

The spell of the stones was broken.

Drng introduced the newcomer to Bork as Lit pill, whose name meant swamp, and which its owner pronounced 'Little' which, considering his colossal size was something of an irony and became the butt of many a cruel jest.

Both Drng and Lit pill agreed that the local tribe had gone into the mountains to hide and would not return until Bork had left. Lit pill then produced another surprise by returning from a short trip into the forest with a girl he introduced as his woman.

Bork was still unsure of either Drng or Lit pill and took each man aside to enquire as to their history under the threat of death if they lied to him.

It took some time to worm the information out of Drng who was reticent as to his past. Eventually he told Bork that he did not belong to this group but had recently joined them to discover the secret of the stone circle, but he admitted he was no wiser as to this than was Bork. His mother had died giving birth to him and his inconsolable father wandered off into the forest when Drng was young and was never seen again. Lit pill came from the same clan which resided on the other side of these mountains. But, he said, he had not seen Lit pill for some time until now, and he had no idea where he had been or why he was here.

Lit pill's story was simple he had been rejected by his group for pestering a woman and had run off with this woman and they had spent the last couple of years teaching themselves how to survive on their own.

The small fighting group needed to rest and to gather provisions for the return trip. And in this Lit pill now surprised them all.

He had kept talking about fish and their use as a food source, and eventually fed-up with his persistence they challenged him to a demonstration.

So, early one morning just prior to sun-up Lit pill and a few interested men set off into the trees. Suddenly they found themselves on the shore of a big lake, the far bank of which was just becoming visible under the lifting mist. Lit pill led them to a small creek, and urged them to remain silent and watch. Firstly he crumbled small pieces of dried meat into the water and before long they were able to see the dark shapes of several large fish swim into the creek after the food. Then Lit pill produced a large sheet of material one edge of which was weighted with tied-on stones. This, with the help of one of Bork's men, he slung across the mouth of the creek, and directing with a wave of his hand they started up the narrowing gap where they then swept up the net with its catch of several good sized flapping fish. Later, back at the camp Lit pill showed them how to clean and cook the catch which, despite its unfamiliar taste, was much enjoyed. Lit pill was applauded.

But before leaving the lake there was an unfortunate incident. Lit pill on the bank lifted his garments round his waist to relieve himself when Drng's tame wolf wandered up and poked his nose up Lit pill's exposed behind. The startled man gave a horrified shout, leapt forward turning as he did to discover the source of his discomfort, danced for some moments on the edge, finally lost his balance, and executing a graceful arc plunged into the lake with an enormous splash.

The men laughed so much they had difficulty helping Lit pill out of the lake.

But the pleasure of this day was short lived.

Long before dawn one of Bork's posted sentries woke him with the news that a small troop of armed men were sneaking through the forest and would be on them very soon. Bork had been expecting this and his defence plan was silently put into operation. His men quietly vacated the camp to hide themselves nearby. Bork had one of his bodyguard-henchmen hold Lit pill's woman under the threat of death if she made a sound.

Then into the quiet dawn a small group of attackers hurled themselves into the camp yelling loudly followed almost immediately by Bork and his men also yelling.

It was all over very quickly, a few attackers realising they were out-numbered fled into the forest leaving two of their number dead, slaughtered without mercy. One of these had been about to spear Drng from behind when a quickly reacting Bork saved his life by running the man through.

Apart from a few cuts and bruises Bork's men were unharmed.

A grateful Drng then gave Bork a real surprise.

Bork had noticed Drng disappear into the trees each day and assumed this was simply for calls of nature. But now Drng asked Bork to join him.

They followed a little used trail for some distance when they came upon a fairly large clearing, green with lush grass, and there tethered to a central post was, of all things, - a horse.

Bork stared in disbelief. He had seen horses in packs and had even eaten their meat, but he had never seen one close up and held like this. He was even more astonished to see Drng walk boldly up to the animal, pat it gently while speaking softly to it, and then with a nimble leap sit on its back and ride it round the grassy space.

The horse was completely under Drng's control.

After this demonstration Drng walked over to Bork holding the horse by the lead.

'In return for my life which you saved, I give you this horse whose name is Flame. And I will teach you to ride him.'

This was indeed a noble gesture.

'I accept your gift in friendship and gratitude,' Bork replied.

Bork proved a rapid learner and surprised his followers a few days later when he rode Flame into the camp.

The dead were taken into the forest by Bork's men where they were simply dumped without ceremony, their weapons being presented to several of his men by Bork. And before they set out on the return journey Bork persuaded the two men to join him and Lit pill ordered his woman to stay with a message for the circle tribe that Bork was now their master and ruler, and they were to destroy the circle of stones.

He would, he said, return - but events were about to take a different shape.

CHAPTER 6

❦ **BORN TO RULE** ❧

*B*ork's troop spent several days getting itself ready for the home trip. Most felt that the foray had been a success and the new recruits Drng and Lit pill had earned universal approval. The former with his young strength and his knowledge of and apparent familiarity with the wild beasts. The latter with his constant good humour at his own many self inflicted disasters.

Drng also proved to be a good story teller and one clear cool evening with everyone except the appointed sentries seated close by a good fire, he told of finding a baby wolf abandoned by its parents and how he kept it warm next to his skin and fed it with crushed dried meat soaked in water to make a weak soup. To his surprise it proved to be a fighter and not only survived but grew very quickly. The growing animal had a natural hunting skill and was soon bringing the odd small gift for Drng to cook and share. They had formed a close bond, and he had named his companion Skill. On hearing his name Drng's tame wolf seated at his side looked up at him expectantly.

Skill was soon accepted by all of Bork's troop but he did have his favourites, of which strangely Lit pill was one. However to Bork's annoyance Skill seemed to not like him and would avoid him if possible. Drng had voiced no explanation for this and kept his suspicions to himself, he had learned that most animals instinctively know who they can trust, and he sympathised with Skill.

On another evening Drng told how one day Skill simply walked into Drng's camp followed quietly by the horse. The horse had stayed and with much trial and error and many a tumble he had succeeded in riding on her back.

It was during this stay that a series of similar events took place which greatly enhanced Bork's stature both in his own eyes and in those of his troop.

In this he began to call himself the Ruler of The Northern Realm of Kingdoms.

They had been there just a day or so when one clear afternoon following early rain, one of the sentries reported a small group of three unarmed males was heading for the camp and would arrive quite soon.

Bork felt the need to impress, so he had a high stool arranged on which he sat with Avilla, Drng and his body guard-henchmen fully armed standing at his side with the rest of his troop arranged in a semi-circle beside them - all very formal.

It did not escape Avilla that this grouping was subconsciously imitating the arrangement of stones that Bork hated so much.

The three visitors hesitated when they saw the troop, but bolstering each other and responding to Bork's beckoning they came forward. Stopping in front of Bork they each gave a little bow, and after a deep breath the tallest began to speak in a clear voice so that all those present could hear.

'Am I addressing Bork son of Tallon, slayer of the standing stones?'

Bork was taken aback by this address, but quickly asserted himself.

'I am Bork. Please state the purpose of your visit.'

'We are of a clan just three,' he held up three fingers,' - day's march from here.' He waved his hand in that direction.

'First - we have heard from a member of the clan that ran from here when you arrived about what you did to the group of standing stones. We are pleased at this action as we also are suspicious as to the purpose of this unnatural thing.

Second - we herewith formally put our clan under your rule, if you are willing to accept this honour, one of us will return to inform our clan.

Third - the two of us remaining wish to join you in your quest to rid the world of this evil.'

A long and pretty speech indeed. Bork was considerably flattered.

'As Ruler of The Northern Real of Kingdoms, I accept your proposition with honour. You may send your messenger after he has fed.

The two who are to stay are welcome, please discuss the arrangements with my deputy and second in command - Drng here at my side.' he waved a hand at Drng and stood to indicate that the audience was at an end.

This sudden promotion of Drng was a shock to him and a kick in the teeth for Avilla who tried hard not to let his anger show and failed. Neither were the troop happy about Bork's choice of an outsider instead of Avilla the long standing local man who knew their history and represented continuity.

This decision would indeed prove to be unwise.

****

Over the next several days five more men arrived, three were from one clan and two from another. They had the same message and Bork took three of them on and sent two back with the message that they too now belonged under his rule. Bork took this to be a universal vote of confidence in him as leader and backing for his ambition to destroy the stone builders. Drng and Avilla in a secret discussion however, concluded that the clans were simply surrendering in order to avoid being overwhelmed by Bork's troop in a fight.

It was only later revealed that the story singers who had visited Bork's clan had followed them north and had observed the whole proceedings from the comparative safety of the forest. They had then moved on telling of what they had seen, of the tumbling of the stones, the final battle, and Bork's victory.

The clans preferred peace to war, and this was confirmed by one of the returning men when accosted by Avilla deep in the forest when the man was on his way back to his home clan.

Bork's troop was now considerably swollen in numbers and he began to worry about provisions. It was however Drng's suggestion that the newcomers earned their keep by forming a hunting party. This was successful and the troop soon had enough to make the return trip.

On their way back a further four men joined them on the same basis as the others.

Bork now regularly referred to himself as The Ruler, and so it seemed to become an established fact. It was, Bork felt, what he was born for, and began to think of conquering the clans to the south to create a single kingdom of The Northern and The Southern Realms, with himself, of course, at the head.

Both Drng and Avilla thought he had gone mad, but kept their counsel.

It so happened that Bork's superiority was challenged on the return trip not by one of the troop but by Lit pill, although it has to be said this was somewhat unintentional. They were camped for the night and as the sun went down sentries were appointed and the rest sat round the fire. It was a fine warm night and the peace seemed to be enhanced by the low murmur of voices. Suddenly Lit pill appeared out of the trees. His normally clumsy progress was however made somewhat worse by his staggering about barely able to maintain an upright motion. To the astonishment of all present he tumbled towards Bork and stood swaying before him. After an effort to gather himself he made a great bow almost falling over in the process.

'Your supreme and royal sir, ruler of the 'kingdoms.' He then belched loudly. 'you claim to be all powerful, but I know you're not......................'

There was a horrified silence whilst all held their breath fearful of Bork's reaction.

Bork also was taken aback and waited to see what Lit pill might say next.

'Ye see your great kingship, I know that yer can't catch fish..........ish..............es, and this humble serv............... erv......hic.......vent can.'

And with this he crashed to the ground at Bork's feet.

Another tense pause, and then the laughter began. Even Bork managed a smile and a chuckle, not sure who was the butt of the jest and suspicious that it was himself.

They put the inebriated man to bed and confiscated the vessel he was still clutching, its contents turned out to be some old fruit juice that had been left so long that it had fermented - hence Lit pill's unfortunate condition.

It was much to Bork's disgust that this hilarious event was, in the fullness of time, added to the story singer's repertoire.

Then just as his men were starting to ask when they were going to return, they had a visit from another group of story singers. The two men and two women were returning north from a long trek south and had an amazing tale to tell.

The four visitors presented themselves to Bork who conducted the usual formalities of introduction with unusual grace. This having been done the spokesman for the singers, who called himself Walther addressed those present.

'We would be pleased to offer you our stories this very evening,' he began, 'but we have travelled a very long way in a short time and find ourselves extremely tired. We fear that we would not be able therefore to do the event proper justice until we are rested. We beg your indulgence and request that you will allow us to sing to you not this evening but that of tomorrow?'

Bork was generous.

'Your request is granted. Our camp is at your disposal to feed and rest until you feel able to join our evening gathering round our hearth, and be welcome. We are all eager to hear what you have to say.'

'We thank you Bork, chief of The Northern Realm of Kingdoms, you will not regret your offer, we have something very special to communicate.'

With these words the four were led away to be fed.

Flattered as he was by the singers reference to his self appointed title, Bork felt his scalp tingle. It was as if he already knew that what was about to take place would seal his future.

Suddenly the relaxed atmosphere of the camp was gone. Tension was everywhere in the air. Unresolved discussions took place all over the place. The natural pessimists looked worried, the optimists seemed exited, the majority were equally concerned but had decided to wait and see - after all it may not affect them at all.

It was in fact to have an impact on all in that place and many, many others.

CHAPTER 7

⇜ **COMMITTED** ⇝

*A*ll were present.

The night noises of the forest could be heard over the crackling of the fire as the men sat round waiting for the singers to begin. As usual they began by introducing themselves, but then they broke from tradition by launching straight into the main story without the normal preamble of lighter songs. All those present felt that the invisible hand of destiny was in charge, its fingers tightening on the future. - After a short converstion between themselves the singers began, but unusually one of the men and one of the women sang together and not in turn as was usual. The other woman had a reed which she put to her lips and when she blew the sweetest notes filled the silence, whilst the second man beat out a rhythm with the palm of his hand on a hollowed out piece of log. The effect of this accompaniment was to enhance the tension until the very air held its breath.

> `We have come a long and weary way our news to tell.
> Strange things have we seen,
> In the south.
> A ring of huge stones as tall as two men,
> As wide as two again,

At this place.
Great stones high in the air, and some laid flat,
Being moved by many,
One by one.
And of another ring of smaller darker stones,
Set outside the other.
Each on end.
Many a man was working on the stone,
Too many to know.
Toiling away.
All and every day this work went on,
Breaking only to eat and drink.
Dawn 'till dusk.
They worked each one of their own free will,
What power that drove them,
We do not know.'

Here the story singers stopped to rest and to let their song take root in the eager minds of the listeners. After some time they clapped their hands for quiet, and began again but this time with a different, tighter rhythm.

'It was as the sun climbed down the sky,
All toil ceased, we knew not why;
The people stopped to watch the sun,
Something strange was just begun.

Men appeared dressed in white,
It truly was an amazing sight.
One raised his hand and all were still,
And all the air a chant did fill.

As the sun's red rim the earth did meet,
The chanting took a different beat,
It lasted till the sun was gone,
Then suddenly there was none.'

There was a pause, then slowly and so quiet they were hardly heard -

'Of the men clothed in white;
They were gone and from out of sight.
They had gone as well they might,
And left to us the quiet of night.'

Now the singers looked tired but clearly had more to say. Sustinance was brought and whilst they drank and ate the listeners fell to discussing what they had just heard with each other, none being able to make any sense of it. But there was more strangeness to come.

Now in the dark, refreshed, the singers then began anew with a bright clear song -

'The next day dawned dry sunny and warm,
We all ate well just after dawn.

What happened then we cannot fathom, stranger things have never been.

Men had baskets made of horn,
Into each were the ears of corn,
Then they crudly walked back forth and threw the contents round about.

The place they did this was aside,
Many strides long and many wide,
   All fenced around we could judge to keep all animals and people out.

The singers stopped at this, bowed to indicate they had reached the end, and were immediately bombarded with questions which they refused to answer pleading to be allowed to meet again the next day.

In spite of his also wanting answers Bork agreed and the story singers left the group to continue asking questions amongst themselves - but without result.

The tension created by the songs affected all who heard them. It was however suddenly unintentionally relieved.

As the fire burned lower Lit pill feeling the cool of the night air had been edging closer and closer to the dying embers. With the flames at his back he failed to notice a loose branch as it fell over the edge. The burning wood caught a loose thread of his tunic which suddenly caught fire and everyone was entertained by the sight of this large person lumbering madly towards the forest and the nearby stream with flames emenating from his backside and bellowing like a stuck animal.

Lit pill survived but his dignity did not.

The next day the camp was in turmoil, nothing remotely like the story singer's news had ever been reported, and everyone was impatient for the evening session to begin. Meanwhile there was some hunting to do and with it now being autumn there was fruit to be found and collected. The camp was busy and the story singers rested.

Eventually round the fire, the evening fine warm and calm, an expectant people waited impatiently for the story singers.

They arrived singly and sat quietly. When all four had been fed and had each been given a cup of hot broth the questions began.

'Who were the men in white?'
'Why did they wait until the sun was setting?'
'Why did they throw away the corn instead of eating it?'
'What did they chant?'
'What were the stones for?'
'Where did the food come from if nobody hunted?'
'Were you afraid?'

So fast and so many were the queries that the singers were overwhelmed.

At this Bork again took charge.

He held up his hand for quiet and got it.

'If you have a question please raise your hand and I will point to a single person and they and only they will ask their question and please keep them short. But first I would like to ask a few of my own.'

A number of hands went up and were then dropped one by one under Bork's withering glare. When all were silent Bork addressed the singers.

'Firstly, thank you for offering to answer our questions, but we do understand that you may not know he answers to some or indeed all of them.

Do you know who the men in white were or what they were about?'

It was Walther who took on the role of spokesman.

'They called them members of the 'Priest Class'. They seemed to be in charge of all activities. One thing was clear they were deeply respected even revered.'

Bork - 'What was the connection with the sunset ?'

Walther - 'They believe that all life is totally dependent on the sun, and they hoped that their chant would cause it to honour them with its warm light in the following days.'

Bork - 'Why did they throw good grain away?'

Walther - 'Of this we are unsure. They said that in due course it made more grain. But this made no sense to us.'

Bork - 'What were the great stones for?'

Walther - 'I am afraid we do not know. They just said simply - 'It's where we meet.'

He added as an afterthought - they said 'It's the law.' We have no idea what this meant.'

Bork - 'Did you see any men armed with weapons,' he leaned forward when he said this as if to stress its importance to him.

Walther - 'No, not a one.'

Bork - 'Thank you for your frankness, perhaps you will answer a few more questions from my people.' He pointed at a man who had had his arm up first. 'You ask your question.'

Man - 'Were you afraid?'

Walther - Hesitated then - 'Not really we were too interested in what they were doing, it was only afterwards when we began to wonder if we should fear them, after some discussion we agreed that they were a peaceful group, definitely not aggressive.'

He was silent for a short while, then - `However if we should fear the magic of the stones or their superstitious beliefs we do not know.'

Bork smiled grimly at this, which added to his resolve to remove this threat from the earth before it had time to take hold.

There were a few more questions of a similar nature, but suddenly the audience were silent, each deep in their own thoughts.

Bork thanked the singers and they and the clan dispersed for the night. For them it had been a new and weird experience, and for many sleep was still a long way off.

Before they left the following day the singers told Bork that they had visited his clan, that all was well there and they had given them the same news songs, with similar reactions.

As the singers left Bork noticed that both Drng and Avilla were missing all day. In fact they had a secret meeting with the singers in the forest away from curious eyes.

There the singers admitted that life at the big stones seemed easier, more relaxed and healthier than anywhere else they had been. In fact the people seemed extremely content. This information gave the two men much to ponder. It seemed to both that they had just learned of a completely new and very different way of life, and perhaps a much better one?

And both men were troubled by the same fear that Bork would wipe out this fledgling new existence before it had a chance to grow and prove itself, but they kept their concerns to themselves - for now.

****

And it was now that Bork found that he had become totally committed to taking up arms against the stone circle builders and the clans of The Southern Realm of Kingdoms. He had clearly been heard to state that this was his intention, but he had thought of it as something to be carried out at some undefined time in the future. Now however, with warriors joining forces with him from other clans a decision on when to start was becoming forced upon him. He also badly needed a plan of action.

His boastful bravado had forced his hand, and he was now unsure of his ability to match the intent with the deed.

Thus it was on a fine warm evening following a successful hunting and foraging expedition and all were happy and well fed that Bork called Avilla, Drng and his two bodyguard-henchmen to a meeting away from the hearing of the rest of the clan.

When they were all seated in a circle each with an expression of worry or puzzlement Bork began-

`What we will discuss here will affect many people and alter the future for the members of many clans.' Here he paused to let this serious message sink in.

`I intend to carry out my threat to eliminate this evil superstitious belief in the magical properties of these stone monuments once and for all. This will mean a long and tough march south, and we may have to fight many battles on the way, with possibly the most serious confrontation at the end. I shall now assume that anyone not with me in this is against me, and therefore will be treated as an enemy. Do you understand?'

The four men, each in turn, said `Yes they understood'

Bork took this affirmation to mean that they were all with him.

This was a mistake. Avilla for one was convinced that the story singers had given them a glimpse of the future and that they should embrace it.

`Winter will soon be upon us. So we must make haste to return home and use the time well to prepare. I propose to set out for the south as soon as the snows have gone.'

Bork, the ruler of The Northern Realm of Kingdoms had declared his clear intention to become ruler of The Southern Realm as well.

Thus it was that their future was set.

The trek home was uneventful, apart for Lit pill on a call of nature in the forest getting himself lost and having to be rescued.

CHAPTER 8

⸂ **RETURN** ⸃

A runner had been sent ahead of Bork's troop to warn those who had stayed behind to keep the homesteads going, of the army's impending arrival. Bork had given explicit instructions not to tell anyone what to expect, warning of dire consequences if they did.

Then back at base there was much excitement, and a celebration meal was prepared. The women especially were looking forward to seeing their men again, and the children their fathers. But none were expecting such a breath-taking surprise.

It was early evening and starting to get cool so a large bonfire had been lit. The trees were still and a crescent moon and a few stars were beginning to show. All sat round the fire and the sound of conversations of expectation floated on the still air. Even the very old and the one sick individual were assisted to places near to the comforting warmth of the fire.

Suddenly they were all agog as Bork appeared from the trees not on foot as was expected but astride his horse. Such a thing had never before been seen and a cry of wonder went up - but more was to come, as Bork was followed by Drng with his tame wolf trotting obediently at his side. At the sight of this the children gave cries of alarm and hid behind a convenient adult. Drng laughed and patted Skill to show that he was friendly. Both Bork and Drng were dressed for battle.

Following just behind Drng came a very lovely young woman who they found called herself Fellysin and there was a murmur of appreciation for her grace and delicate beauty. These were followed by Avilla, Terck and Sollin carrying their weapons of war. Next were the recent additions to Bork's troop also resplendently armed. And finally came the men folk from home simply looking eager to be back with their families.

But the very last to arrive, and on his own, came Lit pill struggling to get his massive girth between the branches that occasionally grew over the path. He burst like a wild thing into the crowd and skidded to a halt only just short of the fire. As he struggled to avoid falling in he wavered about for a few precious moments teetering first on one foot then on the other trying to maintain his balance and only just made it. A sight much enjoyed by the onlookers.

Such was Lit pill's character that he seemed not to be embarrassed but to enjoy the joke with everyone else.

A grand celebration followed and lasted until dawn and until every one had heard all the stories several times, especially the tumbling of the stones, and Lit pill's antics were described over and over again giving rise to much laughter with the man himself joining in.

Bork was honoured by many a fine speech of welcome with much praise for his bravery and his achievement. His self appointed title of Ruler of The Northern Realm of

Kingdoms was considered to have been well earned and he was cheered after each plaudit.

Not to be left out, the members of the force were also made to feel like heroes and much appreciated the adulation.

It was a glorious and happy occasion.

****

And the future waited.

CHAPTER 9

⊰ **BANISHED** ⊱

*T*he journey home had been almost without incident, but an unusual meeting made a fateful impression on Drng.

They had been marching through the forest and were well into the second day when one of the two forward scouts and route finders returned. He was half carrying and half supporting a young woman who he said they had come across wandering half delirious with hunger and all on her own. On questioning her, she said that she could not remember why she was on her own, and had no idea where she was, nor where her home was. All she could remember was that her name was Fellysin, which in her clan meant Raven, a name that seemed appropriate as she had long jet black hair and a smooth well kept skin burnt to a pale brown by exposure to the elements. Although a little emaciated from a lack of food she had nevertheless a singular, almost mystical beauty, which she carried with great dignity. She had the self possession of one who was high born.

In the instant he took to notice this singular woman Drng felt his heart leap in his breast and knew instantly and totally that he wanted her. He felt it with every aching part of his body. His passion was obvious to everyone, and especially when he showed great concern for her welfare.

So they took Fellysin with them and she became a much loved member of the clan. She also proved to be resilient and quickly recovered from her wanderings and lack of sustenance; but she never recovered her memory. Her mysterious appearance was an added attraction to Drng who made it plain to all that she was his. They became inseparable.

The clan also took Drng to their hearts and the children especially were taken with the boisterous Skill his tame wolf. The animal would sometimes allow one of the smaller lads to ride on his back. Drng would admonish them and remind them that Skill was still a wild animal and as such could be unpredictable.

Bork realised that Fellysin was Drng's weakness, information to be stored for possible use in the future. However he was now preoccupied by another problem - Avilla. When he saw the manner in which his mother Chine and Avilla greeted each other on their return he suddenly saw that which he had missed so very many times before, and cursed his stupidity when it also became clear to him that their relationship was common knowledge to the rest of his clan.

He forced himself to contain his anger and growing hatred of Avilla. He felt it was the final insult to his father. However Chine was much cherished and respected by the clan, and so Bork knew that he had to deal with Avilla discretely.

But - Avilla, he decided, had to go.

If he sent him away now Avilla would be facing the oncoming winter on his own and this thought cheered him, he even hoped that the detested man would not survive.

They had been back a few days when Bork arranged a private meeting with Avilla away from any curious ears. He had his bodyguard-henchmen Terck and Sollin being nearby in case of trouble.

The day was dismal, damp and depressing. Moisture dripped relentlessly from the trees and wet feet were the order of the day. Everyone was heavily wrapped and only left their fires in an emergency. Even the young were irritable.

When at last they were alone Avilla saw from Bork's expression what was coming and greatly feared for his future but waited for Bork to begin. He had in any case made up his mind to take his chances and go south perhaps even to join the stone builders, but he would have chosen to travel in the spring.

As they faced one another Bork did nothing to hide his revulsion and spoke through clenched teeth.

'Now,' he said, 'I cannot tolerate your blatant relationship with my mother. I have thought that perhaps you killed my father in order to take her. You must see that I cannot lose her, she is too important to the clan and of course to me.' Here he paused before passing sentence on Avilla.

'Therefore you will leave the clan to go where you will, and she Chine will stay.' He looked at Avilla and was shocked by his tolerant expression.

'There will be no discussion, you have till sunset tomorrow.'

Avilla nodded, and without a single word turned and strode purposefully away. Bork was suddenly taken with the feeling that it was Avilla not himself who had won the day. And instead of being elated he found that he was quite depressed. He had to acknowledge that Avilla had been true to his word and had helped and supported him in his rise to leadership of the clan - he would miss him.

Suddenly Avilla turned to face Bork while still in earshot and spoke so quietly that Bork almost didn't hear.

`You are a fool Bork. You have no understanding of the dangers hidden in what you have set your mind to do. This you may live to regret.' He then vanished in the trees.

Bork's moment of triumph when he had entered the camp riding majestically on his horse had evaporated.

When Avilla returned and announced his intention to leave, Bork arrived to an air of deep gloom. Avilla was considered to be a moderating influence on Bork's ambitions and was much trusted. He would be greatly needed in the days to come. Most blamed Bork and all feared for the future.

However at this point Lit pill, well intentioned as usual, relieved the tension of the moment.

He had been showing some of the children and a curios ring of women how to make a kind of broth from some left over meat. He held the contents in a large drinking vessel which he placed on the ground beside himself whilst turning to scrape a space for it in the embers of the fire. A youth seized his opportunity whilst Lit pill's attention was elsewhere to drop a live frog into the broth. It was at the moment that Lit pill took hold of the pot to place it in the fire that the frog chose to leap out of the liquid and make its escape. Everyone enjoyed what happened next.

Lit pill gave an enormous shout and hurled the pot into the air where its contents sprayed out covering Lit pill's head and chest in a sticky brown mess.

An appreciative cheer went up, and for the moment serious issues were forgotten except by Avilla and Chine.

No one, not even Bork objected when Avilla spent his last evening and night with Chine, and to avoid the sadness of his leaving Avilla was gone before dawn. Concerned friends gathered around Chine to comfort her whilst the company of Bork was avoided as much as possible in that very close environment.

A small seed of power had entered Bork's soul where it germinated, put down roots, and began to grow to fill every conscious and unconscious aspect of his being. He was driven by a force of great strength and persistence, a force that commanded and drove him.

He became convinced that his was a crusade to save his way of life - the old way of life - his father's and his forefather's way of life. He and he alone would rid the world of this new way with its stone monuments and strange unfamiliar beliefs.

With all the vigour he possessed he set about planning to march south with a small but well disciplined army. His aim was to set out in the spring when the snows had gone. In the meantime he would train his troop and put in place what plans he could.

Firstly he got his men together and took them hunting on long hard treks, aimed at establishing his military authority, toughening the men, and providing food enough for the winter and enough for the trip south.

This stratagem was a success and as the snow went Bork had a fit, well trained troop, all of whom were now eager to prove themselves.

****

Bork was however saddened by one aspect of his clan relationships, that was that his mother, Chine, avoided him as much as possible and when they did meet she showed her anger at his treatment of Avilla. She even told him that his grand plan was cursed.

A worried Bork sought to know the future by consulting Zapallor whose words had so often proved to come true.

It was late one night, pitch black with clouds hiding the moon and the stars. A good breeze was about and the stirring bare branches gave noise so their words would not be overheard.

Bork was always uncomfortable in the soothsayer's presence. It was as if she knew more about him than she would tell.

But he began right away.

`Tell me old woman, will my venture be a success?'

Zapallor, didn't need to ask what he meant , Bork's plan was common knowledge, but she fenced.

`How will you measure success?' She asked.

Bork hid his annoyance.

`Will I destroy the stone builders?' Clear enough, he thought.

Zapallor looked hard at Bork.

`I see large stones that are intended to be upright but are lying down.'

Bork was desperately looking for assurance so he took this as confirmation of success.

'Do you see my return?' Bork then asked.

Zapallor took a long time before replying, then -

'That I cannot see, it is hidden,' she paused. 'But what I can see is that you will die by your own doing, but not by your own hand.'

They stared at one another.

'I will die by my own doing, but not by my own hand? What does that mean?'

Zapallor's face clouded.

'I am sorry.................it is not given to me to know.'

At this the old one sat back to indicate that the interview was at an end. She had had to concentrate and was now very tired. If she had other knowledge she did not divulge it.

An unhappy Bork thanked her begrudgingly and left to ponder what he had heard. He continued to worry about the ancient one's words, without coming anywhere near to understanding them.

Now in spite of their care for secrecy Zapallor's prediction became clan common knowledge, and in spite of much discussion the meaning of her words became no nearer to being understood. It seemed that only in its own time would her prediction come to be.

****

In early spring a good warm spell took control of the weather and Bork and his troop prepared to leave. By common consent one of the elder men who had recently suffered a minor fall was nominated to stay behind as temporary clan leader in Bork's absence, assisted by Chine. There were just enough clan members, who for one reason or another were to stay behind, to keep a viable clan presence.

The departure day dawned clear and bright, the air still crisp from an overnight frost. Zapallor stated that the omens were as good as they would get, which fell short of the blessing the travellers would have liked, but was deemed good enough.

There was a great contrast between the staying and the leaving. The former stood silent, some - not just the children or the women - with tears. The others now looked quite formidable, dressed for war, fully equipped with their weapons, gathered together in a noisy column, checking their equipment with each other, as they waited for Bork. When at last he did arrive he seemed made to lead. Seated on his horse his small stature and his short leg were hidden from view. He appeared to be equal to anything and his men gave him a ragged cheer which he acknowledged with a generous wave of his hand.

He turned away and followed closely by Drng with his tame wolf at his heel, and his two bodyguard-henchmen, led the way into the forest. A group of men and women, including Drng's woman Fellysin, were the last to be seen as the trees swallowed them - and then they were gone from view, their voices gradually dwindling away to silence.

Soon however clan routine resumed and life in the home place picked up from where it left off. As ever the imperative was survival.

CHAPTER 10

⇜ AVILLA ⇝

*A*villa was fortunate. It was of course Autumn when he was expelled from the clan by Bork and he was now facing the winter travelling alone. He knew the chances of survival for a single individual in harsh winter conditions with no permanent cover were slender at best. But after several days of following indistinct tracks which seemed to be heading south he literally stumbled upon two travellers. He burst into a small glade and fell over the feet of a tall man lying back in front of a newly lit fire. Another was seated on a log also facing the fire. Taken as they were by surprise at Avilla's sudden appearance, they reacted swiftly to defend themselves. Avilla slowly rose to his feet and facing the men held out his hands to show he was not armed. The men relaxed and asked him to be seated, which he did.

'I am Avilla from Bork's clan.'

'We have heard of Bork,' said the man whose name was Jedd, 'and of his claim to rule all of The Northern Realm of Kingdoms, and of his ambition to rule The Southern Realm also.'

The other whose name was Greth was curious.

'You are a long way from home and appear to be heading south and even farther away from home; and yet you do not seem to be lost. This seems to me to be quite puzzling. If you are who you say you are, then what strange event brings you to this place and on your own? An action which seems like folly to me.'

Avilla told it as it was, and the men recognised the truth of his words.

It turned out that he had accidentally met a pair of story singers who had come from the east and north and were now heading south.

'We have heard of the clan with the great stones and have a strong desire to see this strange place.'

Thus with this declared common purpose they and Avilla joined forces. They welcomed an extra pair of hands, and were duly impressed by Avilla's hunting skills.

After a day's rest the three men packed up and headed south.

Avilla was certainly glad of the company, and the two young singers agreed that Avilla's wisdom and experience were assets which clearly enhanced their chances of survival.

The threatened snow held off and they made good progress. After several more days and nights they reached the white land. Everywhere around them where rocks and stones broke the earth's surface they were white giving the world a lighter, more gentle look. Behind them now was the harsh world of dull brown hills. In the deep valleys they followed there were even some late flowers growing beside the streams giving some welcome living colour to the scene.

Eventually, early one morning just as the sun was beginning to add colour to the day, they came upon a pair of children playing hunting games in and out of the trees.

This boy and girl, wary at first, soon took to the singers and led them to a broad open grassy area busy with people and dotted with living huts.

Almost instantly they were surrounded by curious people, adults and children, all wanting their questions answered. A well-built, dark skinned male shouldered his way to the front with much good humour, and introductions were effected. He was, he said, head of the clan and his name was Herik, and he bade them welcome.

Later that day the story singers regaled the clan, with Avilla amused to hear of himself in song; but it was the following day that serious matters were addressed.

Herik showed the travellers an area some distance away where a large circular ditch was being dug with the earth dumped on its outer edge to form the beginnings of a tall banking.

'I have heard of the stone circle builders and we hope that this will be the foundations of our own much smaller circle, I already have men looking out for suitable large stones,' he paused looking very pleased with himself. 'However work has stopped now for the winter.'

At this Avilla looked grave. 'I have for you a dire warning,' he said, 'soon there will be an army marching here from the north headed by Bork who claims to be Ruler of The Kingdoms of the Northern Realm.'

He paused to let this sink in.

'His ambition and that of his army is to destroy the stone builders and their way of life and to establish his rule over the Southern Realm as well. I have been exiled from the clan for opposing him and his works.'

Herik looked equally grim.

'Then let him come, we will fight him to the death.' Was his simple response.

Avilla smiled unhappily.

'Fine words, and an equally fine ambition,' he said, 'but I would council a different strategy. I suggest you pretend to be on his side, even to the extent of offering one or two men to join him on his march south, they could act as spies. But of one thing I am certain you must keep him from seeing these works.' Avilla waved his had at the circular ditch and mound, the foundations for a stone circle that when erected would one day become Herik's pride and joy.

'What you propose is against everything I stand for,' replied Herik looking doubtful, 'but you know more of this than I, and I shall heed your council, for which many thanks indeed.'

Before Avilla and his companions left they saw Herik call a meeting of the elders and appraised them of the pestilence that was on its way. Their reaction was forthright and unanimous - they would stand and fight. Herik however knew his job as leader and soon had them seeing things his way. He even got his two volunteers to join Bork's army. A work gang was given clear instructions to hide the path to the diggings and to hide them as much as possible from curious eyes.

The following dawn burst on the clan with brilliant sunshine lending optimism to the three travellers as they set off south with many good wishes and as much provisions as they could carry.

But the fine weather did not hold and all too soon the snow arrived and the trio had to give all their attention to their survival. After a brief search they found themselves in a cave, cold, unable to escape for the drifts that were piled against the entrance and desperately short of food with little chance of hunting.

Their spirits flagged as they lay listlessly trying just to stay alive as days and nights followed one another uncounted. It was a trial of individual strength and each was alone with his own thoughts and wondered if they would survive.

Jedd, the slighter and much the younger of the three, slowly slipped into a coma and in an attempt to save him Avilla lay beside him sharing what coverings they both had. They had almost given up when Avilla was roused from sleep by water dripping on his face. The snow was melting. Sadly they could not arouse Jedd and as the sun finally streamed into the cave he died quietly still attended by his two companions.

Weak though they were when the snow had finally gone Avilla and Greth buried Jedd's body in the cave under a pile of loose stones with quiet ceremony.

Avilla too was suffering badly, the wounds he had suffered at the hand of Tallon had begun to cause him much pain, and his years were beginning to tell. It took all his willpower to stay alive.

Greth somewhat younger than Avilla was well built and strong, quite capable of setting out alone and surviving. But he was missing Jedd, it was as if, he said, he had lost an important part of himself. He had however developed a deep liking and respect for the older man and refused point blank Avilla's half hearted suggestion to leave him and make his own way - he would, Avilla said, make better progress.

For his part Avilla had grown to like this unassuming but tough young singer. To while away the long hours in the cave the two men had related their histories, and Avilla had learned that Greth had never known who his father was. He suspected that his mother had been the victim of a rape of which he was the result. His clan had taken care of him until Jedd turned up looking for a companion story singer and began to teach him the skills. He turned out to be a quick learner and after a tearful goodbye from his mother, the pair were on their way.

When Jedd lost consciousness the two men in the intimate atmosphere of the cave shared many confidences, and then one evening which seemed longer than most Greth produced a reed pipe and as darkness drew on began to play. The sweet light notes of the pipe soothed and mesmerised Avilla, and he persuaded Greth to teach him. Avilla, to his surprise found that music came naturally to him and he was soon inventing his own melodies.

It became obvious that the pair would pass well as story singers and to this they agreed.

Then Avilla took a step he had been contemplating for some time.

'Greth, I would like you to think very hard about a proposition I wish to put to you,' he began, and before Greth had chance to reply he went on, 'I would like you to be my son, and for the future you may look upon me as your father and I shall be to you all that a father should.'

Greth did not hesitate .

'Thank you for this most kind and honourable offer, which I accept with nothing but grateful thanks,' he paused, 'and I will always try to be to you the son you would want.'

And so it was.

And eventually the snow was gone.

And the pair then hunted and fed and got on their way as Jedd would have expected.

To Avilla's delight they were everywhere received as a two man story singer team with him accompanying Greth on the reed pipe as he had been taught. It very quickly became second nature to them both.

****

The welcome they had received from Herik's clan was repeated many times as they made their way south, visiting a small clan here and a larger one there. However just a small distance to the north and west of Herik and sited just on the boundary where the brown stone turned into white the two travellers had just missed a small group and this was to have disastrous consequences for this clan when Bork's army arrived with their demands. This clan had became isolated from the rest as winter set in and the snows arrived and so were not warned.

Avilla and Greth's warnings of what was to come left a trail of fear and anxiety behind him as they slowly covered the miles - heading south all the time.

Their spirits rose each day as the weather improved and they regained their lost strength, enabling them to make increasingly better progress. And in truth they soon began to enjoy their self imposed life-style.

Avilla even began to find a little optimism. He hoped passionately that his warnings would not go unheeded.

CHAPTER 11

⚜ **BORK MARCHES SOUTH** ⚜

*S*pirits were high as the army under Bork's command set off south convinced they would either win over or conquer the clans of The Southern Realm of Kingdoms, and return home rich as Bork had promised.

Their reasons for joining Bork's adventure varied with each individual. A few, both men and women, saw it as a way of getting away from the daily routine, of interrupting the monotony of simply fighting for survival. Some thought Bork was mad but had joined him so as not to be left out of any spoils he might win them. Others were there because of deep clan loyalty to its leader. At least two wanted to see more of the world than their immediate environs. A theme common to all to a greater or lesser degree was a sense of adventure, of a journey into the unknown.

Of this ragged group, not yet welded into a fighting machine, only one man was certain of its purpose and was determined to succeed - Bork. He knew that win or lose this trip was his destiny, and knew he would return a hero, acknowledged master of both Realms. This ambition had invaded his mind and his soul, and it was in control.

They made slow but sure progress, and then obvious need for discipline gradually turned the loose straggly group into a working unit with jobs allocated and carried out, and as a result the distance covered each day increased. The people gradually got used to taking orders and carrying them out without too many questions or even, as was the case at the start - refusing.

Bork was forced to accept that a small number of the original starters had deserted during the long dark nights. He felt that on balance he was better off without them.

He was gladdened by that fact that from time to time one or two individuals, mostly men, appeared out of the interminable forest declaring a desire to be allowed to join him. He took them all on after a brief check as to their motives. In this way the army's numbers remained roughly stable, and unwilling members were gradually replaced by committed ones.

Bork had established Drng as his second in command with Terck and Sollin, the two bodyguard-henchmen, in authority under Drng, thus giving the outfit a formal stucture.

****

After several day's marching, the troop reached the place where the dark land was gradually replaced by white, when one of the forward scouts returned to report coming across a small clan. These people sited a little distance off the track seemed to be busy constructing a large earth circle of the kind built to receive the now familiar standing stones.

This was the clan missed by Avilla on his way south and they had no knowledge of Bork and his army nor of its fell purpose. This mischance was to result in the tragedy that was to follow.

After closely questioning the scout, Bork got his leaders together and laid out his plan - his objective to persuade the clan of his cause, if necessary by brute force.

For the first time it was down to him to plan and carry out a successful attack, and he was well aware of the kudos a triumph would bring him, and he recognised the loss of prestige he would suffer should he fail. He worked out his plan carefully and discussed it with Drng and the bodyguard-henchmen. As a plan in isolation it was fool-proof, providing everyone did as instructed.

He hoped to use a complementary combination of surprise and force, a well known and often well proved strategy. His intent was to surround the clan stealthily using the cover of darkness and the close woodland. Then at very first light they would launch a coordinated surprise attack overwhelming the group by sheer weight of numbers of armed men. He placed one squad under the command of Terck with instructions to go left round the half completed earthworks, and another squad under Sollin to circle right, whilst he and Drng would head the central advance. Women and supporters were to stay some distance back. They were to move silently into position in the night and advance in concert at the instant the edge of the sun broke the horizon the next day.

The actual trigger for the advance was to be the sound of an imitation cock's crowing, at which he expected his three groups to move in together capturing the clan to the last man.

It was by anyone's judgement an excellent plan and it would have worked but for an act of pure chance.

Unknown to Bork and his men surprise was lost as a couple of night hunters from the local clan, moving through the surrounding forest with a stealth that only experienced hunters can adopt, came upon some of Bork's troop. They were not detected and made haste to warn the clan. These two were truly frightened as they told of what they had seen. There were armed men everywhere - as many as the stars in the night sky they said trembling. They were scarcely believed, never before had such a large well equipped army been witnessed. Small fighting groups were common but this overwhelming force was something new.

Their chief was duly frightened for his people, and assessed correctly that his chances of winning in a straight fight were slim at best and seized upon his only alternative. They must flee to safety. Thus he issued immediate instructions to pack and be ready to move out before sunrise but as soon as there was light enough to see. They would head up the track which rose at a gentle angle to the top of the nearby mountain and occupy the hill fort at its edge which had long been prepared for such an eventuality. Once here they hoped to prove to be impregnable and he hoped that this army would need to move on very quickly and leave them in peace.

But they reckoned without knowing Bork's will to force them into submission and admit him as their ruler.

The next day was the beginning of a long and desperate struggle between two unequal but determined forces. It was to delay Bork thus loosing him the initiative.

As a blood red sun flooded the area with a dread light, both groups moved as planned. The clan packed quietly in the night and just as quietly set out for the fort as soon as they could see, and reached the path to the fort without rousing a single member of Bork's troop, who were confident they had the situation under their control.

Bork's plan also worked perfectly, as at the call of the cock his coordinated troops swept into the arena yelling and waving weapons. The place was deserted, the only sign of life being a wisp of smoke rising from the now unused hearth.

The small clan carrying two of its elderly members on hastily prepared stretchers were well on their way to their hill fort.

Bork's fury affected everyone and a grand search was made for the missing clan.

They were of course soon spotted when they became silhouetted against the sky on cresting the ridge. Bork waved a useless fist at them and sat down to think.

Later, smoke was seen rising from the fire lit in the fort as the clan started the job of settling in to what they hoped would be a very temporary home.

Bork realised correctly that the clan had not had enough time to collect sufficient provisions to last them for any significant period. Thus, if he could not overcome them where they were he would lay siege to them and starve them into submission.

He therefore warned his people that they might be here for a lengthy stay and set them to establishing a camp at the place of the earth circle.

The following day he sent a small troop under Drng to investigate where the clan were hiding and assess their vulnerability to a direct attack.

Drng returned with the news that the clan had established themselves in a well constructed fortification. It stood at the tip of a natural steep sided rocky outcrop, two of its three sides were protected by vertical cliffs and the third side was defended by a deep ditch and a high stone wall. The only entrance was narrow and well defended. It was, he said, in his judgement impregnable without severe loss of life to the attackers.

Bork accepted Drng's assessment, if he couldn't get them out then he would keep them in, knowing full well that they would be forced to leave eventually for lack of food.

He could wait.

So Bork set a siege with watchers to warn him of any attempt the clan made to break out.

His camp settled down well, but there was no doubt that he had lost some respect as a leader and some grumbled at having to stay in this place where they were strangers and might themselves be attacked in revenge or by a group intent on rescuing those hiding in the hill fort.

His people were also unsure about the earth circle. It might have magical properties which would obviously favour the recent occupiers.

Most avoided the area as much as possible and Bork announced that he would make the clan destroy as much as they could before he left.

And so Bork settled down with his mixture of soldiers and supporters many of which were unhappy about Bork and his strategy.

It was around the fourth day of the siege that an incident occurred that was to alienate Bork from some of his followers, nearly cost him his life, and create an impact that would surface before the end of the adventure.

CHAPTER 12

⇜ **THE FORT** ⇝

*L*ife in the hill fort was almost immediately difficult. The small group of escapers soon realised that they were equipped for just a few short days, and then only if the weather continued to be favourable. But sadly for them a cold spell accompanied by heavy rain showers overtook them on their second day. It was also windy and it even proved difficult to maintain a fire.

Water they had in plenty from a small spring just inside the wall of the fort, but of food and firewood they had only that which they had carried from the base. The vast plateau on the edge of which was sited the fort was a barren wasteland of peat with just a scattering of short scrubby trees.

It was in fact a most inhospitable place.

They were quickly made aware that if the invaders did not leave in four or five days they would have to give themselves up or die of hunger and exposure where they were.

But the first day was fine and warm and optimism was high. They had food which they rationed equably and a good fire. They even had some shelter against the prevailing weather from the walled ditch.

Then after the rain came on the second and the third days some voiced the view that they might be better off surrendering and taking their chances.

The next day everyone was cold tired and very hungry, and a revolt was imminent.

And during all this time they could look down the hill and see with envy the smoke rising from Bork's, previously their own, encampment

Their chief made his mind up, but to preserve moral he told nobody. He had in fact decided to hold out for just two more days.

He knew that Bork held all the cards, he had little with which to bargain, but he was determined to try. He selected his two most trusted men and taking them aside gave them the responsibility of negotiators to go in advance to Bork to see what if anything they might save from the situation. Both men said they would try but confessed to having little or no hope.

Hunger had by now taken over completely. Every single person dreamed all the time of things to eat. One or two of the smaller children were now showing signs of acute starvation.

The position in the fort was now becoming critical. If nothing was done soon they would start to die anyway. Perhaps they had nothing to loose by throwing themselves on Bork's mercy.

However - in the event any initiative was negated by an action and its consequence that was beyond their control.

CHAPTER 13

⸙ **THIEF** ⸙

*E*ven in the comparative comfort of Bork's well managed camp all was not well.

To begin with people were not sure why they were still there, after all the local clan had been defeated and had abandoned their home. Bork had demonstrated his power and authority over them so what more could he possibly want?

What if anything was to be gained by further action? They had joined to go south and here they were stuck in this inhospitable place and in bad weather too.

If they didn't move soon the summer would run out and they would have to over- winter en route, which no one wanted, especially Bork.

With time on their hands, camp politics and divisions began to emerge, and most began to become aware of a for and an against Bork split. A - lets stay and finish what we have started faction, versus an - it's not worth it, lets leave it and go.

However Bork knew that the fort was impregnable and thus to comply with his expressed intentions he had to wait for a surrender. He did not know what provisions the clan had accumulated at the fort but knew that there was a limit and it would eventually be reached.

Also the inclement weather was on his side.

In true command style he decided the answer may lie in creating distractions. To this end he co-opted Lit pill who proved to be a natural organiser and inventor of games.

All instantly took to his unassuming and somewhat accident prone personality, and did there best to join in whatever strange event he came up with.

It could be said, perhaps with some truth that he was the inventor of the egg-and- spoon race, albeit with round stones held in forked sticks.

Three-legged races were also his idea.

He arranged wrestling bouts and a host of other challenges.

Each evening as they sat round the fire he asked for a volunteer to stand up and tell an invented story.

He even persuaded Drng to demonstrate some of the tricks he had taught his tame wolf Skill to do. Skill's performance was faultless and impressed all who were fortunate enough to be there.

Lit pill was appreciated by everybody especially Bork who thought he was an absolute treasure.

And so a few days passed amicably enough.

But the peace was not destined to last.

****

It was on about the fourth day of the siege.

The rain had ceased, the wind had dropped, and it seemed a bit warmer.

Dawn in Bork's camp broke to the noise of an angry fight, accompanied by much shouting and cursing. Suddenly a red faced Terck appeared with a struggling youth in his tight grasp and was propelling him unwillingly forward into view.

The noise woke everyone and the struggling pair were very soon surrounded by a curious crowd which eventually broke to allow Bork's presence as he arrived.

Bork immediately took control of the situation.

He addressed Terck. 'Who have you got there?' He asked.

Terck shouted at the youth to stay still then told Bork what had happened.

'I was on guard duty when I caught this miserable person stealing food, both his hands were full of our food, as you can see he still has some in his mouth,' reported Terck, and threw the crying lad to the ground where he knelt with his head touching the earth.

He was trembling and plainly very frightened.

Bork addressed the boy. 'Is this true?'

The lad nodded.

Bork's fury overflowed. He grabbed the axe Terck was carrying, and before anyone could intervene he brought it down full force on the boy's exposed neck.

It took two blows of the axe to sever the head.

A stunned silence followed, interrupted only by the sound of Lit pill being sick.

No one spoke as people slowly turned away from the dreadful scene, leaving only Bork and Terck standing by the bloody corpse.

Terck was too stunned to move.

Bork, now icily calm, ordered Terck to assemble a small gang and take the body away and bury it. The head he ordered to be taken to the entrance to the hill fort and then for it to be thrown to the clan.

With this act everything was different.

In Bork's camp it was realised by all that Bork really did mean war with all its attendant horrors, and a more sober atmosphere prevailed. The pro and anti Bork factions became consolidated, although the anti's kept their thoughts to themselves.

In the fort on the hill, the sight of the boy's severed head made it plain they had no chance, and they began to make arrangements to surrender.

Later that day a two man delegation was intercepted on its way into Bork's camp and led before Bork.

Bork's terms were harsh.

'We are short of women, therefore we will select those we require, and you will surrender those chosen to travel with us.'

He paused to let that sink in.

'Next, you will each swear allegiance to me as your ruler.'

Pause.

'Finally, you will have nothing more to do with the stone-circle builders, and will immediately destroy this circular mound.'

'Your alternative should you not accept these demands will be death.'

Bork then just stood and waited.

The two men knew that to the clan this would be bitter fare.

'Your terms are understood, and we will convey them faithfully to our chief and return soon with our reply,' said the tallest of the two. And with that they turned and made their way slowly towards the sloping track and the hill fort.

Their chief and the adults in the clan gathered fearfully to hear Bork's terms.

'We have no choice,' said the chief very simply, and turned to organise the return of his, now Bork's, people.

He called the women together and suggested that they said their farewells now and prepared themselves for whatever Bork had in mind for them. He pointed out that at least they would retain their lives, which he had not expected.

'I know this is surrender, but do any of you have a better suggestion?'

The answer was, of course 'No.'

Later that same day the local clan made its way slowly down the slope and approached the arena.

To be fair to Bork the first thing he did was to have the children taken care of. And they soon recovered and were being entertained by a delighted Lit pill.

Bork wanted to avoid any chance of interaction between the two clans and gave orders for his group to move out to a camp some distance away warning of severe penalties for anyone caught fraternising.

When both groups were settled he had the women from the clan brought before himself, Drng, Terck and Sollin. He then asked each to make a selection, and they did. Dismissing the rest Bork addressed the four.

'You have the honour to join us and will assist us in our task. When it is over and we have succeeded you will then be free to stay or to return as you wish.

The women looked at each other in amazement, they had not expected to be so leniently treated.

Soon their sadness at leaving their families was alleviated to some extent by new friendships.

But Bork had chosen one with a hidden lethal intent. She was in fact the only one glad to have been chosen.

She was called Noon.

Noon was young but with a mature figure, dark and outstandingly attractive, she faced the men unintimidated. Her dark eyes flashed as she regarded Bork with hatred, but nevertheless she calmly joined the other three. Bork was for the first time in his life deeply attracted. The stirring in his loins could not be denied, and he immediately established his ownership of her. She would one day be his in every sense, he reckoned, and his heart raced in his breast as he thought about it.

But Noon harboured a bitter truth. And the other three honoured her silence.

CHAPTER 14

❦ REVENGE ❧

*B*y now everyone wanted to be on their way. The members of the local clan had sworn their allegiance to Bork and he had given them his instructions. They had even, if somewhat reluctantly begun to fill in the earth circle that had taken much sweat and toil to create.

But on the very day they were due to start Bork became ill with severe stomach pains. He lay grey and sweating, his face contorted with each spasm. Next day he seemed worse. He was however much taken with the captured woman Noon who each day and well into the night nursed him, mopping his brow and bringing him drinks.

As each day passed Bork failed even to rise from his cot. Strangely, it seemed, he was the only person taken ill.

Then quite suddenly Bork realised the pains began a short while after he had eaten his mid-day meal which he insisted was brought to him by the self appointed nursemaid Noon. He liked to gaze upon her and in his half waking moments, dream about seducing her.

It gradually entered his mind that someone might be trying to poison him. So, on Drng's suggestion he appointed one of the other captured women to act as his food taster.

At first nothing changed, he lay pale and almost unable to speak, but slowly at first and then with increasing speed the spasms receded, and Bork began to shout orders at everyone - a sure sign of his imminent recovery.

This realisation, that someone was trying to kill him, made Bork suspicious of nearly everyone, all that is except the attentive and seductive Noon.

What all the captured women knew and had sworn never to divulge was that Noon, the source of Bork's blinding passion, was no other than the mother of the youth that he had beheaded.

Skilled in the knowledge of the forest Noon had selected certain fungi, the juice of which she obtained by crushing the caps, and surreptitiously dribbled into Bork's food.

She knew that it was undetectable, accumulative, and would eventually lead to his death. In Bork's love sick mind she could do no wrong, and he even convinced himself that her ministrations were because she returned his aching obsession.

Bork had survived. But Noon was patient and her revenge could wait.

Bork never suspected that what he had taken in and now cherished was a very lethal and determined snake.

****

The year was now showing unmistakable signs of the approaching autumn. The leaves on some of the trees were beginning to turn a rich golden brown, and there was fruit and nuts in great abundance.

They must find suitable quarters before the winter and Bork needed to be much farther south by then. He therefore set the group to making preparations to march. He now felt reasonably well and was cheered by the thought of leaving this place of unhappy memories. Unfortunately just before leaving something happened to disturb Bork's peace of mind, but was to end by reinforcing his resolve.

It arrived in the shape of two story singers from the north and with news of Borks clan he had left behind.

They were keen to get on their way as soon as possible and so their songs were brief.

> 'We have seen those clans far to the north,
> Where Bork the ruler now holds forth,
> They are doing the work that He declared,
> No effort in complying was ever spared.
>
> Bork with his tame horse Flame,
> Deeds have won him fame.
>
> But of his own clan we can tell,
> All we saw was not well.
> Good and bad together came
> Fate declared it was to blame.
>
> Happy some who would rejoice,
> At good news we now give voice.
>
> A joy we found which pleased the tribe,
> Tallon's wife and Bork's mother -
> The fair Chine is with a child,
> And celebrations were full wild............................'

'No!....................No!' Screamed Bork at the top of his voice.

At this the singers stopped and looked stunned, whilst everybody present stared at him in shocked surprise.

Bork ground his teeth, cursed, and spat out with great venom just one word -

'Avilla.'

Then very quietly and with great determination - 'I vow by my ancestors that I will kill him. Wherever he is I will find him and finish his life just as he finished my father's.'

He turned, his face contorted by hate, and strode away from the group.

It was only then that it was realised by the rest that Avilla was the only one who could possibly be the child's father, and that either male or female the new born would inherit the position of head of the clan after Bork.

The visiting story singers had expected this to be received as good news, and were at a loss as to what to do next.

It was left to Drng to bring the session to a close after asking the singers what the bad news was.

'It was simply that the group are missing the troops and were concerned that they had had no news of you for some time.'

'Thank you for that,' responded Drng, 'please stay and enjoy our hospitality - we will talk further in the morning.'

The following day Bork had recovered from his shock at the news and he and Drng sat down with the story singers to discuss their own and the singer's future intentions.

As the singers declared their intention to continue south, Bork realised that as they would travel much faster than him, he could use them to warn clans they might come across on their way that he intended to conquer those who would stand in his way, but he would welcome into the combined Realms any who would surrender. He reasoned that this strategy might work against him, but hoped that the singer's reporting of the size of his army, their confidence and organisation would cause them to be shy of a battle which they would almost certainly lose.

He even advised them that his ultimate destination was the grand stone edifice he had been told was under construction, and he suggested that they who dwelt there might send a message by means of story singers who were heading north as to whether they were with him or against him.

The singers looked grim at this news of war, but respectfully reminded Bork that they regarded it their duty to report events as faithfully as possible, and this would certainly include Bork's dire warning.

With that the singers thanked Bork for his hospitality and gift of provisions, and left.

****

Bork was now aware that there was dissent in his troop, and called them together to unite and to rally them.

Drng and the bodyguard-henchmen rounded up the whole troop which had now grown considerably since the start. Collecting them all around him Bork was impressed and confidence grew in him that he would achieve his aims.

He mounted his horse to gain stature in both height and authority, and to leave no doubt in anyone's mind that he was chief.

And thus from a small piece of higher ground he addressed them.

'Tomorrow we march,' he announced.

There was a ragged but uncertain cheer. Most were glad to be doing something.

'We will go south as far as possible before the snows come.'

There was a few groans from those who thought they might be heading home.

'I need you all with me, every single one of you has a role to play in this fight for our way of life. With you behind me I know we will succeed. We will unite the two Realms and in this we will be laying a sound base for the future, and for all our people.'

More convincing cheering raised his spirit.

'You will be sung of as heroes, and our ancestors will thank you.'

At this there were loud cheers.

'And if fortune is on our side, which I'm sure it is, we may all return home richer than we could dream.'

More cheers and shouts of 'Bork the ruler.'

'So then, my friends, let us set to with good hearts.'

Bork raised his hand in salute and dismissal.

And with this the crowd broke up and a spirit of well being and co-operation grew as the people began their preparations to travel into the future and the unknown.

Only one small problem occurred, one of the women claimed to be pregnant and pleaded to be allowed not to go on. Bork asked who the father was, and on being told sent for him.

'Are you the father of the child this woman is carrying?' He demanded.

'Yes,' came the simple reply.

'Do you accept responsibility for them both?'

The man had to accept.

'Then you have a choice - either way it will not be easy. You can stay as part of this army and we will try to look after you but that will be subject to our commitment. Or you can leave and find your way back to re-join our clan or another.'

At this the pair moved out of Bork's hearing to discuss the issue.

They didn't take long.

'Thank you, we will stay,' said the man, and the woman nodded her agreement.

****

The following day broke warm and sunny. But in spite of an early rising it took a long time for the whole group to be ready, tents, kit and provisions all packed up and slung on someone's back. The delay meant that the distance covered was less than they had hoped, and by late afternoon the advance scouts reported that they were approaching what appeared to be the territory of a quite big clan.

They had stumbled into Herik's home ground.

Warned as he was by Avilla, Herik set out to welcome Bork and to convince him that he was on his side and shared his views. His tribe had been lectured and the circle mound and its paths well hidden.

Herik had prepared a large space nearby for Bork's camp. He hoped and was assured that Bork would be on his way again the following dawn.

The army unpacked little, Herik had promised to feed them, and they soon had eaten and settled in for the night.

CHAPTER 15

❧ HERIK ☙

*B*ork was tired. He was still feeling the debilitating effects of his poisoning, and was grateful when Herik suggested that just the two of them should retire to his hut where they would be fed by his woman and could talk without being overheard or interrupted. Desperately afraid that Bork would discover that he was opposed to the ideas behind the army's intentions, Herik offered his personal hospitality to their leader. It was early evening, but already quite dark as the nights were drawing in, when they were settled together, and Bork warmed by Herik's hearth and well fed, began at last to relax. The gentle human sounds that arose from the group of huts gradually quietened as the pair lay back on piles of soft furs. Herik had his woman bring them drinks of slightly over mature fruit juice, and as the alcohol took effect, Bork now very much at ease began to talk. And talk he did. He began to release a deep need to explain his ambitions and his motivation behind them. Herik listened fascinated, and eventually, unable to help himself began to query Bork's convictions.

It proved to be a fascinating debate, wasted by there being no means of recording it, and equally sad when on awaking both Bork and Herik could remember little of what was said. They both remained convinced in their own beliefs.

Bork began -

'You know Herik, It's a hard task that I have set myself....... and to succeed I must believe that I am right.' he paused and Herik waited.

'It is certain that I, and only I, have the drive and ambition to do what must be done. I know by the blood of our forefathers that it is my destiny.

'I will either win or die in the attempt.

'I find it hard to accept that the people can throw away our whole way of life for some crazy new idea.' Herik did not respond.

'Why is that Herik?'

'It might just be better,' was the quiet reply. Herik was very concerned not to show his hand.

'In what way better? What is wrong with the present way? Is it not built from many past generations of trial and error? Is our present way not the best that we can possibly achieve?

'We have come such a long way. We have learned how to use the seasons to our advantage. We have learned how to hunt successfully, and even thanks to men like our Lit pill, to catch and cook fish. And with men like Drng we will all soon be travelling on horses.'

Here Bork took a swig from his beaker and sat back in thought. He was so silent and for so long that Herik thought that he must have fallen asleep.

Then suddenly rousing himself Bork began again.

'We have good sound dwellings, and we know how to protect ourselves from the worst weather. And we can even save many a sick person with herbs and potions passed down to us by our parents, and their parents before them. Must we throw this all away for some kind of magic?'

Herik could no longer resist and threw in his hand.

'But can we not keep all of this and accept something of the new way as well?' He suggested very tentatively.

'Possibly,' said Bork, 'but will we be allowed to?

'I see the power behind this new way, these stone erectors, these scratchers of the ground want to force their ways on us all. They want to unite us and then rule us. And if they succeed where will the knowledge and respect of our ancestors be then?' He paused for breath.

'Do you think they will let us be free? Their influence is growing fast. I have seen it with my own eyes on this march, and I have heard it, as you must have from the story singers............

'No it must be crushed before it is too late.......'

Herik sighed, this seemed to him to be all one sided. Hesitatingly he countered -

'But they don't seem to want to go to war their activities are peaceful.................'

Bork jumped in.....

'That's the danger if we don't stop them by force they will take over by expanding their false beliefs, and our clans not knowing any better will fall into their trap.'

'But as far as I can tell, these people only believe that the sun brings forth all life and this process can be helped by man.'

'Can we believe that? They claim that a single seed of grain if placed in prepared ground it will grow into many such seeds. This sounds like powerful magic and superstition to me.' Bork was too tired to show the anger he felt.

'But,' said Herik, 'we can surely try it for ourselves - what have we to lose?'

'There you are,' said Bork, 'if we did that we would be starting to give in to them - a chance we must not take........

'Soon they will be clearing the land of its trees to provide prepared ground and then what will happen to our game - it will have nowhere to go, thus taking the very food from our mouths.'

Herik paused for thought. He dare not mention his little trial patch of prepared and planted ground. He had to tread very carefully indeed.

But before he could respond Bork began again, somewhat wearily now.

'And what is the meaning of all these circles of stone. They must believe they hold some invisible power or why put so much effort into them?'

'The only power these stones have is that which a man believes to be in them. They are a symbol of permanence, a permanent place, a place where decisions can be taken, news announced, and clan rulings be discussed and agreed, a place of law and of control, and even a place of ceremony and of celebration.'

Herik had spoken with passion, and quickly regretted doing so. He felt he might have given himself away.

But Bork replied mildly, 'Well said. But you are wrong. The old traditions are still the best and I promise you I intend to wipe out these new ways once and for all.'

For a while Herik said nothing.

Then very quietly -

'But you can't stop people having new ideas.'

But Bork didn't hear him - he had fallen asleep.

****

The following day Bork was roused by the sound of much activity outside and with a sore head. Herik's woman brought him a bowl of life warming gruel, and for once Bork forgot about his food taster.

Leaving the hut Bork was gratified to find that Drng assisted by Herik had everything under control and the troop was all ready to move out. Herik led Bork's horse forward and helped him to mount. Bork looked around checking everything then leaned down and held his hand out to Herik, who promptly grasped it firmly in his own.

'Go well, my friend,' he said, 'may our ancestors protect you.'

'And you also,' replied Bork.

Herik found that he had tears in his eyes, in spite of having opposing views he had come to like this man. He liked his strength, his drive and commitment, he felt that he stood head and shoulders above other men. He also liked him. But he felt strongly that he would never see him again.

At that moment he could not have said on whose side he was.

For his part Bork liked Herik unreservedly and promised himself that he would return to this place and they would spend many an evening in serious debate.

Then just before they moved out two men stepped forward. They were fully equipped for war and for travel. They approached Bork and requested they join him promising him their support on Herik's behalf.

Bork thanked them gravely and waved them to join the troop.

These two were in fact the spies suggested by Avilla who proceeded to weld themselves into Bork's ever growing army. They were not detected.

Herik stood alone for a long time gazing into the trees where the last of Bork's troop had so recently vanished and the sounds of their passing had finally died away. Heaving a great sigh he turned and made his way back to the world he knew and cherished. He felt that a great storm had passed, but its wind would be felt for some time to come.

Would the life they had been used to ever be the same again? He thought not. He knew in his mind that Bork was wrong but his heart would yearn for the old ways.

Back where the huts stood and people moved about busy with their own concerns, Herik dismissed these thoughts, he had a clan to be a father to.

Father was right - he had just been told by his woman that she was with child - and of course he hoped for a son.

Herik's first task was to organise a gang to clear the hidden way to the 'field' and to the circular mound, which they would continue to prepare for the stones already earmarked to be brought and erected. The 'field' had been 'sown' with grain in the spring and was now beginning to show a satisfactory mass of ripening plants which swayed and bobbed in the breeze.

As he arrived at the 'field' to organise the harvesting of their first ever crop, Herik gazed at their achievement and felt a great wave of sadness for Bork but especially for his people and those he might injure in his blind drive to satisfy his ambition.

That evening Herik's clan celebrated not just their harvest but also Bork's departure. It had been a tense time and now they were able to relax and be themselves. It proved to be a joyous night and many a praise was heaped on a much embarrassed Herik.

At one point he held up the proceedings and spoke to all who were present.

'I thank you for your kind words, but please let us remember that without Avilla's timely warning all would not have been well. I thank him from my heart, and wish him well wherever he might be.'

This short speech was cheered, and the celebrations continued far into the soft autumn night.

CHAPTER 16

⁂ **WARNINGS AND PREPARATIONS FOR WAR** ⁂

*A*s they made their way south, deep into the land of The Southern Realm of Kingdoms, Avilla and his newly adopted son Greth were finding it harder and harder to convince clans that had known nothing but peace for at least a couple of generations that a terrible scourge was on its way to overcome them and to re-establish the old ways.

Most groups declared that they would temporarily surrender and return to their own ways when Bork moved on, and thanked Avilla for his timely warning. Avilla even got used to singing his caution in true story singer style.

But Avilla was particularly concerned about Bork's declared final objective, the grand circle which was the capital of The Southern Realm. He feared that they would never capitulate and without an established fighting force they would be overrun, leaving Bork to rule over both Northern and Southern Realms.

He knew from the story singers that Bork was still marching south and feared they hadn't much time to find some defensive force.

It was still autumn and the pair were making good progress which if continued would see them at the big place before the winter. If, and it looked likely, Bork was held up by winter weather they might have until the spring to prepare for the battle he feared would come.

Then a chance meeting changed their plans.

They were making fast progress along a good wide track when the came upon a couple of men in a sun dappled glade busy preparing a meal. They were immediately made welcome and introductions were effected, they too were story singers who were on their way north having spent the summer at the grand circle.

Avilla and Greth were fascinated by what the two had to tell of the massive work being undertaken, and of a very different way of life.

The singers told them that Bork's movements and ambitions were known to this very sophisticated southern clan. Singers from the north had warned them.

However, of one thing they were very clear - on no account whatsoever would they give in to Bork and his troop, which they regarded as an untutored and uncultured rabble from the north; this said with apologies to Avilla.

It grew late and as the light faded all four pitched tents and retired having agreed to spend the next day deciding if there might be a way to prevent what looked like being a bloody victory by Bork.

Left alone again Avilla and Greth agreed that someone should go east and try to recruit an army of sufficient size as to provide a decisive support for the circle people.

They also agreed that this should be Greth, leaving Avilla to continue on south so as to further warn the clan and assist them by using his intimate knowledge of Bork and his strategies.

It was dull and a light drizzle was dampening both things and their spirits as Avilla explained their plan. The others then took a short while to discuss matters between themselves and to Avilla and Greth's delight suggested they would split up and one of them, Joonry the elder of the two, would join Avilla to speed his journey south, whilst his companion, Hapt, would go with Greth to help in recruiting an army. They were to join up at the great circle in early spring.

So after eating and packing up, hands were shaken, well wishes spoken, Avilla gave his adopted son a hug, and these good men set off in different directions and were soon lost from view from each other in the trees and the fine rain.

The weather was noticeably colder - they were running out of time.

****

As it happened, Avilla and his companion made good progress and were within striking distance of the great circle before the snows came. They had however no luck in convincing anyone of the danger about to engulf them.

****

Greth and Hapt meanwhile were having a tough time of it, and more than once were on the verge of giving up. Their first encounter and attempt at persuading someone to join them was typical of many.

They arrived at a small group of earth huts. There was an air of steady activity about the place, At first they were not noticed, but when they were they were made welcome as story singers always were.

Relaxing round the evening fire they began to sing of Bork's siege of the hill fort and of his cruel beheading of the unarmed and starving youth. They sang of his large army bent on subduing all they encountered. Their warning was bleak and to ease the tension they sang of Lit pill's invented games.

In the morning they met with the elders who thanked them for their timely warning. They would post advance sentries and retire deep into the forest where they would prepare a winter camp, and wait until the army had passed through. They would leave nothing at all by way of food or clothing for Bork to steal. This they hoped would encourage the troop to move on quickly.

Greth approved this strategy, but when he asked for volunteers to build a defensive force to hold the grand circle they got no response, for which the chief apologised.

The two shouldered their disappointment with their packs and set off to try again at the next clan.

However their persistence eventually paid off as a number of good strong individuals agreed to join them. These were mostly unattached men who were looking for a bit of adventure, some relief from the clan routine. A decent sized force was accumulating when an unusual situation in which they found themselves set them right back to the beginning again.

The small force headed by Hapt stumbled on a larger clan than they had come across so far.

To Hapt's surprise they were welcomed by two youngish women instead of the usual male elders. Nevertheless they were equally hospitable and set about providing sustenance for the troops who were by now arriving behind Hapt.

Whilst the women got busy Hapt and his men began to realise that there seemed to be no men about.

It was Greth who asked where the men were, and was told they were out working 'in the field'.

On further questioning the women explained that oddly only female children had been born to the tribe for some considerable time. Now the women outnumbered the men by many times. The clan by now was made up of nearly all women.

The visitors regarded this situation with some glee, and looked forward lasciviously to the evening's entertainment round the fire. And when it came they were not disappointed. They had never before seen such a fine collection of young, eager females - most of them unattached and eager for a partner temporary or permanent.

It was a dream come true.

And the men set to with a will.

The result of this unfortunate meeting was that in the morning Greth and Hapt set out with just two of those they had so patiently recruited. The rest stayed behind to take their luck with the women. This was of course good for the future of the clan but almost a disaster for our pair.

It took all their available will power to set out again, and by now the first flurries of snow were in the wind.

The climate this far south was somewhat milder than they had been used to and although there was some quite heavy snow falls it did not lie long on the ground, thus they were still able to make good progress.

Their persistence paid off and as the year turned they had again collected a small army of disparate adventurers which Greth tried his best to weld into a disciplined squad.

The trouble was that they were used to making their own rules and taking their own decisions and found that taking orders or instructions was very much against their nature, and would insist on arguing about every move.

Just as the year turned they still had a long way to go to reach the great stone circle.

They were running out of time.

Then as they turned south west the weather suddenly got much worse. It snowed for several days and forward progress was halted.

Food became scarce.

The men began to complain.

'This is not what we joined for, to be starved to death, and to be frozen in our cots,' they said.

'Then exercise your famous tracking skills and fetch us some meat, and also bring some logs to keep a good fire going,' Greth admonished.

But they would be going nowhere until the heaps of drifting snow had all but vanished.

The weather did not let up and despair set in.

They barely survived.

It was well into spring when the lying snow allowed them to continue. The winter had taken its toll and most were weak from a reduced diet and stiff from too much inactivity.

They did heir best to hurry but Greth and Hapt felt more and more that they would be too late

By now Bork would be well on his way.

CHAPTER 17

⚜ **WINTER QUARTERS** ⚜

*M*eanwhile Bork and his troops smashed their way south, overcoming all resistance and demanding loyalty to Bork. Fortunately injuries were slight and there were no fatalities.

Inevitably with such a loose and mixed group organisation was poor and the resulting progress slow. It gradually became clear that as winter was fast overtaking them they would soon have to bunker down somewhere safe until spring.

It was Bork's plan to arrive at his target, the great stone circle, in the coming spring. He had not thought any further, and had no idea what to do when he had captured the place other than to destroy the edifice and with it all the superstitious nonsense he hated so much. And with it of course Avilla should he be found there.

But he had succeeded so far and his confidence was high. And as is often the case over confidence led him into trouble.

It was late in the day, which had proved to be balmy, They had covered a good distance since dawn with only a short break for food and drink, and were somewhat tired. The attention of the two front scouts had drifted as they chatted together, their minds being on a woman they had agreed to share but who had as yet not agreed to this arrangement.

Suddenly they came on a wide cleared space with several living huts dotted about. It nestled in the broad curve of a river of considerable width, and appeared to be deserted.

The instant they saw this there was much yelling and cursing behind them. Turning and rushing back what they witnessed was mayhem. Bork's people were rushing about in a blind panic as stones and boulders rained down on them fired from a host of slings.

The perpetrators of this well planned and executed ambush were well hidden in the surrounding trees and shrubbery. The barrage lasted for several minutes, then as their ammunition ran out, several well armed men ran out and proceeded to attack any solitary or isolated member of Bork's now panicking force.

In all of this only Bork kept his head. High on his horse he swirled around thrusting here and there with his javelin and roaring orders to his men at the same time. Slowly, one by one, the attackers disappeared into the trees and order was restored. It was then found that the body of one attacker lay dead and apart from almost everyone having been injured in some way by a missile, two of Borks men had also been killed.

When his troop was lined up and ready to proceed Bork had the two scouts brought before him and in front of all admonished them.

'Do you have any excuse for such a disgraceful lack of attention to your duty?' He asked.

One of the two spoke up.

'We just did not see a sign of them, they were so well hidden, sir.'

'As scouts you have proved useless, therefore I am reducing you to the level of ordinary soldiers.'

He allowed his anger to subside.

'It would have been better if you had died instead of those who did and for who's death we shall all hold you responsible.........

'Dismissed.'

This sentence was the worst he could have chosen and both men were suitably subdued. But the one who had spoken ventured again.

'Sir, with respect - I do have something of some importance to report.'

'Well,' said Bork.

And at this the man hesitatingly told of the group of huts ahead and of the river.

This news cheered Bork somewhat. This might just be what he was seeking as his winter camp.

'Right..........But finally you two will arrange the burial of my two good men and that of our enemy before sunset today.'

With that Bork not wishing to be taken by surprise a second time posted sentries. He then led the troop forward into the cleared area and stopped at its edge to survey the scene. It was better by far than he had hoped for and immediately gave orders for them to settle in.

Sometime later all was in order and the two men reported that burials mounds had been prepared near-by for the dead, Bork's two and the attacker. At this Bork gave a clear order for all present to attend the burials, and as they stood quietly around Bork told of their bravery as fighting men and of his respect for them as members of his troop. Each of the bodies were then laid in the shallow hollows together with their weapons and the people quietly dispersed. The bodies were then each covered with earth and a low mound of stones piled on top.

The loss of the two fighting men affected the group badly. In such an intimate society as Bork's small army both were known to everybody and were much liked. Both were men who were always at the front of any hard task and always willing to assist anyone else where help might be needed.

There was a general air of gloom about the place, recovery from which looked like being slow.

This air of despondency was not helped when it became clear that in spite of the increased vigilance of the posted sentries men from the home clan would manage to filter in through the trees and lease off a barrage of missiles only to vanish again as secretly as they came.

Hits were frequent and soon there was no one left without some small injury, including Bork who had a nasty gash on his forehead. Relaxation was impossible and people stayed under cover as much as possible.

However the raids stopped with the first fall of snow which meant that the attackers could now be easily tracked and eliminated. After which hunting began to be successful and moral began to improve.

****

A couple of days after they arrived Drng returned from an exploratory trip upstream to report finding a wooden bridge spanning the river via a small grassy island in the middle.

Bork, Drng and the two bodyguard-henchmen went to investigate Drng's find. It had been worrying Bork for some time as to how they were to make the river crossing when spring came and they would continue south.

The structure was neat and minimal. It was simply a pair of long and fairly wide logs laid across the water so that one end was resting on the bank with the other on the small island. The upper half of each log had been chopped away to leave a flat surface to walk on. Hand support was provided by stout branches forced upright into the river bed at intervals alternately on each side of the logs. A similar structure lay from the island to the far bank.

They each tried it, and although it sagged a little in the centre they found it both easy and safe. Its drawback was that it would only carry one person at a time making them vulnerable to an enemy.

They wondered why the home clan had left the bridge intact and guessed that it was an inducement for them to be on their way.

The next day it snowed heavily and continued on and off for the next several days, and with the enforced lack of activity with only essential work being undertaken - moral started to drop again. Old grumbles re-surfaced and there were some unpleasant exchanges.

Bork especially became depressed as in spite of trying his hardest to please Noon, he realised that she was avoiding him as much as possible in that confined space. Unfortunately this merely inflamed his passion. This situation was made harder to bear by his constantly seeing Drng and Fellysin together and clearly deeply in love. He did his best to ignore the issue but it was quite obvious to even the casual observer how he felt. He decide that if his feelings were not returned then one day he would take her by force. He still had no idea that Noon was still looking for an opportunity to kill him. Besides, she was gradually becoming aware of her growing affection for, of all people, Litt pill. She had come to recognise that his foolishness was simply a disguise for his shyness beneath which lay a wise, sensitive, and very intelligent man.

When it eventually stopped snowing the weather turned quite cold and the surface of the snow which now lay thick and in large drifts became frozen so that although one could walk on it every now and then a foot would break through throwing one into the deep snow, much to the amusement of any onlookers.

Bork had them clear the area on which the huts stood, but yet again it was Lit pill who saved the day, and as usual began the proceedings by making a fool of himself.

Between the huts and the river the ground sloped gently downhill, just steep enough for what the ever inventive Lit pill had in mind. And although it was cold a bright sun shone down and the snow glittered with a thousand tiny diamonds.

Taking an old unwanted skin he started out for this slope.

This small act was so unusual as to cause the whole camp to follow him, curious as to what madness he was about to indulge in this time.

At the top of the slope he placed the skin down with its plain side on the snow and its furry side uppermost. Then lowering himself on to it and in a sitting position he grasped the two front corners of the skin and using his weight he slid forward onto the slope.

What happened next was spectacular. The skin with Lit pill still seated on it hurtled with increasing speed down the slope. He yelled with exuberant joy as he slid down the slope going far too fast now to be able to stop before reaching the waiting river.

The watchers cheered him loudly as he descended but gasped when it dawned on them what must inevitably follow.

Still clutching the skin Lit pill shot out over the river and entered the water with an enormous plash.

Fortunately for Lit pill the water was only waist deep and a loud cheer went up as our hero surfaced and struggled to the bank where a dozen of pairs of willing hands were outstretched to assist him.

He was helped and cheered all the way up the slope, dry clothes were found and he was parked as close to the fire as safety permitted.

Very soon a snow barrier had been built on the river bank to prevent further un-intended duckings. Many unwanted skins had been found, and racing competitions down the slope were soon in progress, and competition was fierce.

That evening round the fire song and laughter rang out continuously, with many a pat on the back for the now warm and fully recovered Lit pill.

The following day he invented snowball fights.

And the day after they woke up to see a human figure sculpted in snow and dressed in Drng's favourite hat. It was a great hit especially with Drng and Fellysin who said it was more like Drng than Drng.

Lit pill! Quite a man.

CHAPTER 18

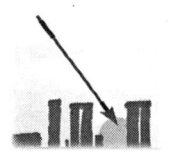

❧ **STOPPED** ☙

*T*o every one in Bork's winter quarters it seemed as if they would be stuck there for ever. In spite of all that they could do to lighten the long wait it was a depressing time.

Petty differences were apt to surface, often unintentionally, and tempers occasionally became difficult to control.

They were all a long way from home and felt it. Worse they were in for another long march and a life or death confrontation at the end of it.

Into these tensions Bork started afternoon talks round the fire when weather permitted. He used these to assess what his troops feelings were, and to drive home the essential message as to his purpose.

In this not once did he mention Avilla's name concentrating solely on removing the perceived threat to their way of life. However, Bork's hatred; some thought fear; of Avilla was known to all and his motives were thus suspect.

By now they had all seen how these others lived and many had realised that their standard of living was in some respects superior to their own. Bork tried to play this down, but could not remove what was obvious. In spite of all Bork could do the attitude of those who had begun to doubt the right-ness of what they were about to do was hardening. An undercurrent of revolt was slowly but steadily brewing.

Into this cauldron a number of things happened to make matters worse.

The first was that it gradually became noticed that two of the men were no longer about. A quick but thorough search ascertained that they had in fact gone missing.

They were Herik's pair, and Bork feared the worst, but they were liked and most people reckoned they had simply got fed-up and left for home. The snow was by now so trodden that their tracks were lost.

In fact they had crossed the river via the bridge and were making fast progress south to warn the great circle builders of Bork's progress and intentions. They carried a full knowledge of the strength and weaknesses of Bork's troop. Information that was potentially invaluable to a defender.

Herik's spies had been activated.

Bork reacted by getting the whole troop together and announcing that anyone else wanting to leave must do so now otherwise he assumed they would be with him to the end of the march.

No one else left.

The next near set back was a second attempt on Bork's life by Noon.

She had noticed that the chief often went for a short stroll in the immediate woods after dark. On one such occasion she took a knife and at a discrete distance silently followed him.

Out of sight of the huts she made her move and lunged at the figure and was about to bring the knife down on the defenceless back when she was startled by the sharp bark of a wolf close-by, tripped over an unseen root and fell with a crash into the snow at the man's feet. She felt a sudden weight on her back and hot animal breath on her exposed neck.

There was an oath of surprise followed by a sharp command and the pressure on her back vanished, and a hand reached down and grasped hers. The hand was not Bork's but belonged to Drng who was taking Skill for some excersise. When he saw who it was he simply assumed she was there on a call of nature. The knife was lost in the snow - she would look for it in the morning.

Embarrassed, they apologised to each other said goodnight, and went separate ways.

Neither told Bork of the incident.

Noon thought that she could wait.

The third thing was much the most serious and affected everyone.

The year had at length turned and the weather became unusually warm. Whilst this cleared the snow from the living area it also created an enormous quantity of melt water upstream of the river. On the morning of the day of the disaster they were startled to be wakened by a sudden loud roaring noise coming from the direction of the river.

They reached the bank to see the resulting damage caused as a huge wave of water had driven with all its force downstream and had taken the bridge with it. They gazed at it with unconcealed dismay. All that could still be seen of it were one or two of the hand poles sticking out of the swirling grey water at crazy angles.

Bork who had been hoping for an early start to his march south now had to rebuild his only means of crossing the river.

More delay. He cursed roundly.

They stood with sinking hearts watching the sad remains of their means of escape.

The following day Bork held a council of war. He laid out what needed to be done and found that there was no shortage of volunteers to do the work. The job was made harder, however, by their not having many tools suitable for working in wood, but they did have manpower so the few axes were used in relays.

By the end of the first day suitable fallen logs had been found in the forest and had been manhandled to the right spot on the river bank.

The attacks of sling stones by the home clan had strangely stopped so the riverside activities continued un-interrupted, and by the end of the next day the logs had been trimmed to give a reasonably flat walking surface on each one. The next problem was to get the logs across the river, firstly from the nearside bank to the island and then the final pair of logs from the island to the far bank. This was accomplished with the assistance of Bork's horse which was used to haul the end of each log across the intervening waters. And at the end of the third day it was possible for anyone with a good sense of balance to cross the river dry shod.

On the last day vertical hand poles were rammed into the river bed at suitable intervals, and when this was done everyone crossed to the far side and back again.

They congratulated each other on a job well done - which it was.

That evening after several ad hoc celebrations Bork ordered them to be ready to move as early as possible the following morning. He also detailed a squad to raise the living huts to the ground and to destroy the bridge as they left to establish his absolute authority.

But events transpired to change his mind.

As they were starting to leave two people appeared carrying a third on a makeshift stretcher, It was easy to see that they were carrying a very ill person. Soon a second stretcher party appeared and then a third.

They ignored Bork and his people, made for the fire, started to tend it and place the sick as close to it as was safe. They took no notice of Bork's people, it was as if they couldn't care what happened to them - as if what they were having to deal with was problem enough.

As more arrived Bork and his squad made ready to destroy the huts, but before they could move Noon appeared and stood between the squad and the living quarters.

`Don't you dare damage a single hut,' she said red with anger, `can't you see these people are sick, you heartless beast.'

`I don't care,' replied Bork equally angry at having his orders challenged, `they should be taught a lesson.'

`Then go ahead if you must,' Noon spat out, `But just think what it will do to your reputation when the story singers start to tell of these events, as they surely will.'

Then - `Go on, do it!' Noon said quietly, `and I shall be the first to spread the news.

And you had better not damage the bridge either.'

Noon stood defiant. Hands on hips she looked Bork straight in the eye. Outwardly brave she trembled inside - she had no idea what Bork might do.

Bork looked at this strange woman who had dared to challenge his authority and thought he had never seen anyone so desirable. His flesh tingled with the thrill of her and he was lost.

After a very long pause in which the many on lookers held their breath, Bork held up his hands and ordered his people to leave everything as it was and to move out. Which they did, leaving two of their women folk who decided to stay and help nurse the sick.

The home clan had been hit by influenza and nearly half of their number died including one of the two women who had stayed behind.

****

Much later, it was Noon's heroic intervention that was sung about by the story singers. Her name became as famous as Bork's.

****

The snow had gone, they had crossed the river safely, and they saw no further obstructions to their march, and morale picked up as they made good progress south and could see an end to the adventure.

There was a veriety of views about Bork amongst his people as the army made its way towards its ultimate goal, a goal they had been pursuing now for over a year.

Some thought he was a great leader to have got them all this far a feat not attempted before as far as anyone knew. A few thought that he was weakened by giving in to Noon, whilst a similar number admired him for his compassion in doing so. On balance he seemed to be still in complete command of his troop and they appeared to be willing to attend his every command. This of course was essential if they were to do what they had spent all this time and effort to do.

Although all were apprehensive about what they would find when they got there, and were totally relying on Bork knowing exactly what he was about.

And some aware of Bork's hatred of Avilla still had doubts as to his real motives.

Meanwhile Bork was still fully committed to establishing himself as ruler of both The Realms and destroying the new ways. Whatever doubts he may have entertained he succeeded in overcoming them. He guessed correctly that of all the forces that abounded in the then known Realms his was by far the stongest.

It was certain that from now on nothing or no one would be strong enough to stop him.

Bork, the boar, and the scourge was on his way. Those who would oppose him should tremble.

There was not a force in the land strong enough to hold him.

He would be ruler of both Realms.

CHAPTER 19

⟮ **ARRIVAL** ⟯

*J*ust as Bork and Greth, in separate places - the one in the west the other in the east, were preparing to settle in for the winter the snows, Avilla was approaching the great stone circle, and even though he had been told all about it by the story singers he really did not know what to expect, not the least because of the superstition and magic that seemed to surround any discourse that involved the place.

He was also nervous as to what kind of reception he would get. He had no army, he was unarmed, a stranger, and from Bork's clan - what could he possibly have to offer.

What might he expect - perhaps indifference at one end of the scale with maybe summary execution at the other.

This place he was coming to was reputed to be the most powerful place known, and he found the prospect of his encounter daunting. It haunted his waking moments and all too often his dreams.

He was both eager to get there and tempted to delay at the same time. But he had no choice, these people must be warned of the scourge that was heading unbendingly towards them. He hoped it might make a difference. In the end that was all he had - hope.

The story singer Joonry had proved to be an excellent travelling companion with a wide experience of people and an extensive knowledge of recent history. He also had a sound sense of the local geography and of which routes to choose for safety and which for speed. However, intent as they were on warning as many clans as possible that Bork was on his way, they took a somewhat convoluted route so as to reach as many people as possible. This strategy also had the advantage that they were entertained almost every day and could thus travel light and fast.

Without exception they were warmly welcomed, and most had heard of Avilla. Joonry was of course already well known as a previously visiting story singer.

On being warned about Bork the reaction of the clans was similar. Most approached the situation practically, and without panic set about agreeing and planning their strategy. These people had probably seen worse than Bork at some time in their history.

So, when it came to how they might deal with Bork, almost all decided to give in and honour him as the new ruler rather than risk loosing a fight and possibly lives. And two of the clans had the same novel solution. They diverted the track away and around their compound whilst hiding the original track that lead directly to their homes. They then posted scouts some distance up the trail to warn of Bork's approach. When they were alerted they slid silently deep into the forest until the army had passed marching harmlessly along the diversion.

All thanked Avilla and Joonry and wished them a safe and speedy journey.

As they got nearer to the now famous place Avilla became increasingly nervous. Joonry who had visited the grand circle in the role of story singer sought to reassure him that he had nothing to fear. But when he went on to describe the hugeness of the place Avilla became even more troubled.

He constantly turned the same questions over and over in his mind -

Would anyone listen to what he had to say?

Would he be believed?

Would his warning be heeded?

What could they do against Bork's trained and well equipped army?

Would he be in time?

Would they fight?

Above all would Greth be there with a newly recruited army of his own?

These doubts and more chased each other through his head during every waking minute.

In the event he could never have imagined what the place and events proved to be.

****

Avilla had actually lost count of the days they had been travelling when he became aware that Joonry was showing signs of excitement.

They had gradually left the forest behind and were now on a smooth much used wide almost straight path. On each side and to their front there lay a nearly level grassy plain. Clusters of huts began to appear here and there. Around these a few people were about, and to Avilla's surprise these took little notice of them. Clearly strangers on the road were a common sight and therefore no surprise to these folk.

At first these hut groups became more frequent, but then quite unexpectedly they found themselves on the very edge of the largest cleared area Avilla had ever seen. The sun had passed its highest point and there was an increasing chill in the air heralding the oncoming winter, but in spite of this the scene was so full of activity as Avilla could never have imagined. All he could do was to stand where he was and gape, much to Joonry's amusement.

There were people everywhere he chose to look. The immediate impact however was not one of a disorganised crowd milling loosely about, but there was a discipline at work. Each individual seemed intent on carrying out a specific and familiar task.

And then, when he saw it Avilla was stunned, for in the distance there appeared an enormous stone construction which was the object of all this energetic activity. It was obviously in the process of being built, and wherever work was taking place it was clearly being directed towards this one great thing.

Avilla noticed that most of the building processes were taking place within visible range, nothing was hidden or secret.

Although far from being complete the structure already dwarfed those working on it.

Enthralled, and quite shaken, Avilla with a somewhat amused Joonry at his side walked slowly towards the centre of the activity. They were not stopped or even, it seemed, noticed - so intent was everyone on what they were doing.

The first thing they passed was a large flat space sheltered from the worst weather by a wooden roof covered by thatch, beneath which a group of men were shaping two enormous stones. The work was demanding. These men sweated freely in the cold air as they chiselled away at the hard stone with bronze chisels. Another group, close by. were constantly sharpening the tools on rough grit stones and swapping them for used blunt ones.

These huge stones when fully prepared were destined to join others already in place in the distance.

Between this stone foundry and the final building another stone of similar size and shape was being hauled by more men with ropes and long wooden poles for levers, its progress eased by its being supported on its back on logs so that it rolled slowly but steadily along. It was being transported with much strain and effort from the shapers and finishers to fit into its own allotted resting place by the side of those already set in their final positions.

As with the other toilers every man appeared to be straining his utmost as was needed to move that massive block of grey stone albeit very slowly, just barely a hand-widths at a time.

There were no slackers, should any one person relax the forward motion would instantly be drawn to a halt. However a rest break was called from time to time to allow the team to recover. They then sat round in a group not talking much, simply resting.

It would take many days to move it to where it was needed, and then the whole process would begin again with the next block.

The two companions passed the stone haulers and now Avilla for the first time had a close and uninterrupted view of the final work.

Astounding as everything had been so far, nothing could have prepared Avilla for the staggering size of the stone circle and its surroundings. Several stones were already in place and where the remainder were to be mounted wooden stakes were hammered into the ground to mark the corner of each block.

The already upright stones were at least as tall as two men and were half a man's height in width. They cast long shadows as the afternoon sun sank towards the horizon. And if that was not hard enough to take in, several of the erected stones were linked on their tops by huge stone lintels. Avilla noted that each lintel was shaped into a gentle arc to match closely the circumference of the final circle.

As they approached there was much shouting and the voices of more people than they had as yet seen. There stark against the clear sky was a massive device of wooden beams and ropes. Men were heaving and calling directions as others pulled on ropes attached to long wooden levers. They were lifting one of the prepared stones into its position where a pit had been prepared for it and into which it would eventually be man-handled into an upright position.

Avilla could only watch, this was building on a scale he had never imagined- it was awe inspiring and it made him feel very small indeed.

As they moved close to one of the upright stones Avilla felt that it must touch the very clouds in the sky.

And so the pair stayed rooted to the spot as the late afternoon gradually darkened into evening and lack of light caused the work to come to a gentle stop and the workers strode away singly or in small groups, and the sound of heavy work dwindled into an atmosphere of tranquillity in contrast to the previous noise and bustle.

It was time for them to meet someone in authority.

Just then, as if in answer to the thought, and seemingly from nowhere suddenly appeared two tall figures unusually dressed completely in white. As they approached the foremost held out his hand in greeting.

Avilla took it in his and looked into the kindliest eyes he had ever seen. Bright blue and caring they appraised Avilla with just the merest suggestion of humour. But his face was creased in a broad smile.

'Welcome,' he said, his voice deep and warm, 'you must be Avilla and your companion Joonry. We are expecting you.'

Taken aback, Avilla could only manage to stammer a thank you.

'I am Sonlith, chief here, and this is Pallin my deputy.' He waved at the very old man by his side. The old man merely nodded.

'If you would care to follow us, you will be taken good care of. You must be weary after your long trek.'

'But we must talk, matters are urgent,' said an agitated Avilla.

'Rest easy my friend, there will be plenty of time for that,' replied Sonlith calmly.

'We know that the problem you have come all this way to warn us of will not reach here until the winter snows have gone.'

At this unexpected piece of news Avilla stopped and stared at Sonlith.

'If true this is good news indeed. Can you be certain, it doesn't sound like Bork to stop for anything?'

'We have been visited recently by two good men from a tribe in the north whose chief they say is one Herik. They joined Bork on Herik's suggestion but left when winter snows halted the march and he settled on the far bank of the great river until the coming spring. You will have ample opportunity to question them in the days to come.'

Avilla felt tremendous relief surge through him. He still had doubts, but if true there may still be time to prepare for the worst.

During this discourse they had been walking slowly, at the pace of the old one, towards a long wooden building with a roof of straw thatch and smoke gently staining the darkening sky from its central hearth.

'I hope you will be comfortable here,' Sonlith said with a wave towards the building. 'You will be joining the Law Givers, of which we are two, and you will be fed and attended by our good women, who incidentally work just as hard as you have just seen the men folk.'

Then, voice full of concern, 'We will not talk tonight, I can see you need to rest.'

Both his guests were grateful for this consideration.

They were shown into the building more spacious then any that either of them had ever seen. Sleeping spaces were allocated to them and almost immediately food was brought. No sooner had they eaten than Joonry fell into a deep and relaxing sleep the first he had experienced for many days.

But sleep would not come to Avilla whose mind still churned with doubts. As he lay in that strange place with questions still chasing one another through his mind, the hut gradually filled as other men entered and after a brief but friendly `Good night' bedded down to sleep.

Eventually he could not tolerate his restlessness any longer and quietly rose, found his shoes and made silently for the door.

Once outside he was immediately struck by the freezing air, winter was well and truly on its way, and he almost regretted leaving his warm bed.

Taking a look around he soon forgot the cold. A huge, clear, and brilliantly lit full moon hung in the sky giving the whole scene an unreal shimmering quality, lacking all colour but almost as clear as day. It made everything seem larger than it really was. Avilla was looking at a black and white exaggeration of the world and was thrilled by the unbelievably magnificent breathtaking beauty of it all. He felt as if his senses could not take any more.

He then gradually became aware of a great certainty that he was meant to be here. It was as if all his questions had been answered by the one vital fact - he was here. This was it, he felt that this place had given him a clear understanding of the formidable task he had assumed. Win or lose, he had to do his utmost to prevent Bork succeeding.

Returning to the sleeping quarters, Avilla's last thought as he drifted at last into sleep was - `Maybe it will be all right after all.'

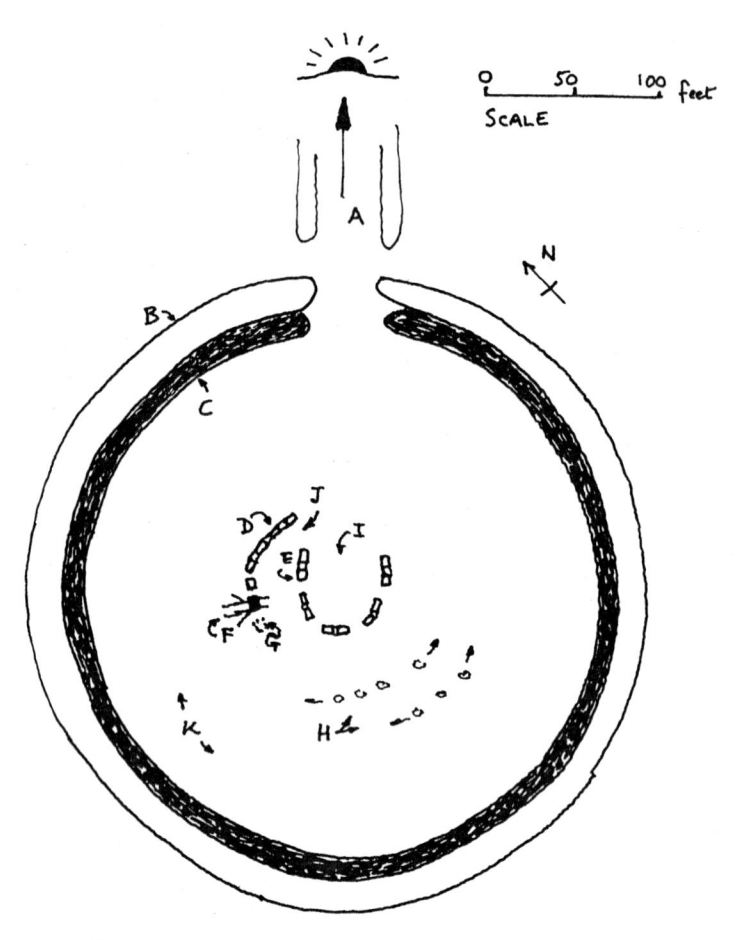

THE GREAT STONE CIRCLE – UNDER CONSTRUCTION
AS AVILLA SAW IT (SEE KEY)

KEY TO PLAN OF:

THE GREAT STONE CIRCLE - UNDER CONSTRUCTION

A. Approach route leading to the entrance. Points approximately to where the mid-year sunrise breaks the visible horizon.

B. Deep circular ditch, the first circle to be built.

C. High earth mound, built at the same time as the ditch.

D. Outer ring of great stones with linking lintels - under construction.

E. Inner group of great stones - pairs linked with lintels - complete.

F. Outer ring great stone being hauled into place and raised.

G. Hole dug ready to take the next outer great ring stone.

H. Two incomplete circles of other smaller (grey-blue) stones being moved to ease construction work.

I. Inner court - mostly for council members only.

J. Middle court - mostly for other involved persons.

K. Outer court - for general use by anyone.

CHAPTER 20

⟪ **THE GREAT STONE CIRCLE (I)** ⟫

When Avilla finally awoke the following day he did so to find himself alone in the big house. Judging by the sounds filtering through the mud and straw insulated walls everyone else was up, out, and working. He emerged to find that this was so, but as soon as he appeared a youth ran up, gave him a shallow bow and spoke politely.

'Good morning, the chief, my master says he hopes you are rested, and would you kindly join him at the morning meal?'

'I thank you,' replied Avilla, 'I shall be honoured, please lead the way.'

Snow flakes were drifting slowly down from a leaden sky, and it looked as if there would be much more to come. It was cold and Avilla was glad of his all-weather travelling cloak.

The lad led them past the great monument of the huge upright stones where, as before, men were hard at work. To Avilla they were no less impressive at close quarters. He shivered involuntarily as he passed, whether or not there was magic here he nevertheless felt a great power was at work.

A question occurred to him which was to spring to mind quite often in the days to come - 'Did the people control the stones or the stones control the people?' It was a question to which he never discovered the answer.

As they strode past the working groups the boy was frequently hailed and he would answer cheerily, clearly he was well known and liked.

'What are you doing with an old man?' He was asked. 'Can't you find someone your own age to play with?' Someone joked.

The lad's reply amused those who heard it, but it was a trifle on the rude side.

At that Avilla realised how much he had missed light, uncomplicated conversation, and suddenly began to feel recent tensions starting to ease.

So strong was the feeling he badly wanted to cry.

Sensing Avilla's emotion but not understanding its cause the boy quietly took Avilla's hand.

And it was hand in hand that they eventually came to and entered a building similar to the other but slightly smaller.

Even though it was dull outside, the inside seemed completely dark, but as soon as Avilla's eyes were accustomed he could see Sonlith seated with several other men and one woman round a warming fire, its smoke gently rising through a neat hole in the roof. They were each dressed in long bleached white robes.

'Thank you Elln,' said Sonlith, gently dismissing Avilla's young guide.

'He is my sister's son,' he added, 'and he has been assigned to you as general guide and helper for however long you choose to stay. Anything you want, or anywhere you want to go just ask him.'

'Thank you,' was all Avilla could find to say, he was bewildered by the overwhelming hospitality he was being shown.

'Now, I trust you are rested,' Sonlith continued, 'your friend Joonry has gone to stay with some other story singers who arrived recently. He especially wished me to say how much he valued your company, and would be pleased to join you again any time. A nice compliment I think.'

Avilla thanked him, but before he could say more a plate of cooked eggs and bread was brought for him which in spite of his hunger he thoroughly appreciated. In fact he had not tasted bread so good in his life, and he managed to enquire about it.

The group had been silent while he ate, but the woman it was who replied to his question.

'Yes,' she said, 'we are rather proud of it. It is made from our own grown grain, which has been threshed, ground and baked here. We normally have some fresh every day, winter as well as summer.'

'Yes indeed,' interjected Sonlith,' but you will learn all that later. We need to talk about more serious issues. Avilla will have plenty of time to see the way we do things here.'

He then introduced the others seated round and explained that these were all the members of what he called the 'Council' who he said made all the group's important decisions, broadly decided their future direction and were the ultimate custodians of 'The Law'. They met both informally, as now, and formally when all serious issues were aired and dealt with. It was, he said, a kind of informal and when required, formal ruling body. Members of the council were selected on merit or their contribution and experience and asked to join. Their white robes merely identified them as council members, they were not regarded in any way as denoting a higher status. He stressed that all were considered to be equal partners in their endeavours.

It was a long speech and created in Avilla's mind a turmoil of new feelings and ideas. He was bursting to ask a whole lot of questions but was prevented as Sonlith smiled at him and said - 'More of that later, it is important that we learn from you of your recent history, what you know of Bork and what you think he will do.'

Avilla looked round at the serious faces and knew how important for these people and himself his words would be, and took a little time to compose himself and consider only those elements of the story that might be important.

And he told it as it was.

He told them about his dispute with Bork and his subsequent banishment from the clan, making it clear to them that he was Bork's declared target and thus would bring a risk of war to whoever was harbouring him.

Avilla then told them of Bork's detestation of what he had heard of this new way of life, represented by the stone circles springing up everywhere, and of his set ambition to destroy it and maintain life as his forebears had lived it.

He told of Bork's ambition to be ruler of both Realms, and his willingness to fight to achieve it.

He paused here to let this sink in, asked for and received a drink of refreshing water.

'Please continue,' requested Sonlith eventually.

Avilla told of his long trek with stops to give warnings, and of his passing the winter in a cave. He was quiet for a time as he related the untimely death of Jedd. He then spoke with pride of adopting Greth as his son, who he felt he had put at risk by sending him east to collect an army in order to defend this place.

'But I have heard nothing of him since we parted,' he said, 'and I have no knowledge if he has succeeded or if he will arrive in time. It is almost certain that he will be held up by the winter.'

He stopped.

'That is all, do you have questions to ask?'

'Yes, I do have one. What do you think Bork will do when he arrives?' Asked Sonlith.

Avilla paused for thought, then -

'He will ask you to surrender or fight,' he said, 'if you choose to surrender he will destroy all your works, disband your group, and set this place back to where it was before all this.' He waved his hand in a broad circle to signify everything around them.

'However, if you choose to fight - and lose - the result will be the same.' He paused, then with great sadness he said, 'It seems as if you will have to fight and win.'

Sonlith was aware of the stress Avilla must be under.

'Thank you, we will ask no more of you for the present,' he said quietly. 'This will need more discussion but it is possible that we have all winter before us to prepare, and we may be in a position to confirm this.' He turned to one of the councillors and spoke quietly to him for some moments, following which the man excused himself and left.

When he had gone Sonlith addressed them all again.

'We are extremely fortunate, thanks to two very brave men to have first hand knowledge of what has been going on in Bork's army. Thanks also to a good clan chief - one Herik, who, at the suggestion of Avilla here had two of his men join Bork's troop. They recently made their way here where they arrived just yesterday.

'I have sent for them and when they arrive we shall all hear what they have to tell us.'

To Avilla this was indeed good news, the ruse he had agreed with Herik had worked, and better than he had dared to hope.

They didn't have to wait long before the councillor returned with two tall athletic strangers.

The pair bowed to Sonlith, nodded first to Avilla then to the rest of the assembly and sat as requested.

'Please tell us of Bork, we need to know all and any information you can provide, but may I suggest by starting with the strength of his force.' Sonlith requested.

Then slowly, each man taking a turn they told of Bork.

They gave a colourful description as to the size of the army, its weaponry, its preparedness, and its discipline. The men, they said, were totally loyal to Bork who had promised them great riches on sacking the great circle.

It was an unhappy council that took in this terrible news.

But they then raised spirits of the assembled group a little.

'So much for facts,' said one of the two, 'but we have surmised the following from simply being there and keeping our eyes and ears open.

'First - there is some dissent in the force, though we don't know how many, but we believe that Drng, Bork's second in command, is sympathetic to the future way of life you offer.

He had secret conversations with Herik. Bork is unaware of this.'

Avilla interrupted 'Yes I can confirm this, Drng has discussed his doubts with me even before I was sent away.'

'Good,' said Sonlith 'Next?'

'We believe that there was at least one attempt on Bork's life, a poisoning, but we can't say by whom - we just don't know.

'Lastly, he had reached the far bank of the great river when heavy snow halted his progress south. He settled in there, and we think it almost certain that he will not march again until the warmer weather has arrived and the flood waters have receded to allow a river crossing.'

Whichever of the two men was speaking the other confirmed his statement with a vigorous nod of his head.

'We thank you again,' replied a chastened Sonlith, 'for the extremely valuable information you have brought to us at great personal risk. I have no doubt as to the punishment you would have received had you been discovered, you would have forfeited you lives.'

He paused.

'As to your future, you are welcome to stay and spend the rest of your days with us or to leave to return to your own or another clan, just as you choose.'

'Sir, thank you, but we joined Bork as fully armed fighters. So if you will allow it we would like to stay and take our part in your defence.'

Sonlith heaved a heavy sigh.

'How can I possibly refuse such a selfless offer, and you are most certainly welcome,' he said.

Then turning to the assembly and assuming a stern demeanour he said, `None of this must reach other ears. Our whole strategy will depend on our maintaining total secrecy.' He then bowed to end the gathering.

With that they all stood and left, all that is except Avilla and Sonlith.

For a long time they were silent each mentally assessing all that had been said, trying to evaluate what it might mean to their ultimate survival.

Eventually -

`So, he's coming,' exclaimed Sonlith.

`Yes, it's inevitable, and he is determined,' replied Avilla, `I hope Greth can get here in time with a good force at his command, I wish I had heard something of his progress.'

They sat in companiable silence for a goodly while.

It then came to both men that they had a deep respect for each other. They were made from the same metal and cast from the same mold. They knew they could trust one another implicitly. This then was the beginning of a friendship that would be beyond place and time.

What Avilla did not know as yet was that Sonlith knew more than he could believe of Avilla's history, and had plans for him.

And what plans! Avilla had no idea as to what was about to happen to him.

Sonlith told himself to be patient such important matters must on no account be rushed.

Meanwhile he would show Avilla the great work that they were undertaking and hope to convince his as to its merit.

'If you are recovered from your journey perhaps you will permit me to be your guide for today. But as you must be aware we expect everyone here to contribute what they are able - I am afraid that this applies to guests also,' Sonlith said smiling gently.

'Had you not suggested it I would have volunteered anyway.' Avilla replied.

They strode out under dull dark grey clouds with just a few large snow flakes drifting gently down in the still air. Work on the building had ceased to avoid, as Sonlith explained, churning the area into a swamp of mud. Only activity under cover was permitted.

'Everyone here has at least two skills for both good and bad weather conditions,' Sonlith hastened to point out.

With that he took Avilla to the central area.

CHAPTER 21

⁂ **THE GREAT STONE CIRCLE (2)** ⁂

'The first thing to understand is that this work was begun many generations ago, too many to remember,' Sonlith began, 'and we, the present custodians are continuing it. It will take this and many future generations to complete. What is certain is that no one here will see it finished. So our toil is an act of faith that it will one day be fully built.'

Sonlith paused to allow Avilla to appreciate this statement, and went on -

'What is it? And what is its purpose?

'Well it's many things. Firstly, I suppose, it is a statement - it says 'This is us, it's who we are and what we are. We have built this to demonstrate that we are here and we are here to stay. Above all it represents permanence as opposed to a temporary, shifting way of life. A fixed place on the land which will always be here to return to - a stable base on which to found a new community.

'Secondly it is a meeting place where all our important decisions are discussed by the council and concluded. The law that rules our lives is laid down here. It is where disputes of ownership and of others are decided. Male, female relationships are agreed and differences settled. And sadly even punishment when deserved is meeted out.

'Here it is that our ancestors are formally honoured, and the dead remembered.

'And why is it designed like it is?' he waved a loose arm in the direction of the stones.

'Well, it is nearly impossible to explain. You see it has evolved over a very long time and each generation has brought their own ideas as to how it should be when finished, and I have no doubt that future leaders will continue to make changes.

'However there are a few fairly stable and fundamental rules, if you like, for the design.

'Firstly, size, it had to be big, massive even, to ensure permanence and to establish authority. It is in these things that others have failed. They have been much too easily destroyed by either man or even adverse weather.

'Second, it has to serve the function of a meeting place for the council which also allows the people, that is any who wish to do, to be able to witness all formal proceedings. Visible decision making is important to us.

'And lastly, but more importantly by far - the sun.' He looked up as at that moment the snow eased and a shaft of warm sunlight broke through a gaping hole in the dull sky and bathed the huge stones in a warm glow almost bringing them to life.

Avilla was taken aback. 'How did you do that?' He asked.

Sonlith laughed. 'I would like to think it was I who caused the sun to shine, but it was pure luck, we could just as easily have been struck by lightening.'

Avilla chuckled, much appreciating Sonlith's honesty.

'But as I was about to say,' began Sonlith again. 'The sun. The sun is the most important natural element in our lives.

'Without it we would quickly freeze to death, our seeds would die, our plants not grow and our corn not ripen. In fact we believe that every living thing needs the sun to survive.

'We have even been told by a rare passing trader of other places where the sun shines nearly all the day long making the people rich beyond dreams.

'So here we respect, and even honour the sun, believing in its life enhancing ability. We cherish it, even love it, we have taken it to our hearts - but understand this we do not worship it.

'There is no special magic built into the stones or its arrangement on the ground that can be turned on or off at will. This is not a place where the supernatural hides.

'However in recognition of our acknowledgement of the sun's vital importance in our lives our ancestors arranged the layout to support our main annual ceremony. The structure now looks out along a line that allows us to watch the sun rise on the mid-year day. It is the one day we express our wishes for the future and give thanks for the past. A few people now come from far away to join us on this happy occasion - we usually have a good feast, I hope you will still be here to join in the next one,' he concluded.

'I thank you for the invitation which I intend to honour,' replied Avilla.

'Good,' thought Sonlith and smiled gently to himself. He had to hope.

'Now enough chattering, let me show you round, it will be more pleasant now the snow has eased off.'

So saying they strode side by side in friendly silence towards the entrance to the circle.

From his very first footsteps that took him into the circle to the very last as he stepped out again Avilla was completely overwhelmed. The enormous size of the place dwarfed anything he had imagined. He felt very small and insignificant as he stood looking up at the central group of stones from the entrance. There was a strength here built into the structure by the uncounted number of days spent on its construction by those who toiled and continue to toil in building it. And it was with a sense of awe, even of reverence that he approached the council area and found that the staggering greatness even power had taken his voice.

Power.

This place created it.

This place held it.

This place used it.

Power. Avilla felt that the word explained everything.

One would have to be very strong willed to commit untruths, or acts of folly whilst being over looked by these massive stones. The experience was chastening, even subduing.

But there was hope here too. The place said here it is, this is the future and it will not falter.

And Avilla began to understand and with understanding began to accept that this was the new way of life, a movement begun in the past, consolidated here in the present, and promised by these stones to be the future.

Standing there with Sonlith, Avilla began to feel strangely to be a part of this place.

He relaxed, and gave himself up totally to studying the construction and the visible building process openly on display.

The council area was the only part fully completed. It was laid out in the shape of a U or like a beaker on its side. Lintel topped columns formed the sides and the closed end, the open end looked out along the entrance way and the wide approach track. It was along this track that the big stones were dragged and were in the slow process of being stood on end in a circle surrounding the inner chamber.

Many people could stand in the space between the outer ring of large stones and the inner chamber and witness the council at work.

The outer ring was far from complete and it was clear that this work would take a very long time, perhaps several generations. It was possible to study the erecting process as the latest addition still had the timber and ropes used to lift its top so that the bottom end dropped neatly into the hole prepared for it. Avilla gazed in sheer wonder at the size but essential simplicity of the lifting mechanism.

Some holes had been dug to take the next upright columns.

The few erected stones of the outer ring had lintel stones joining them together.

Several smaller stones of a very different type and colour lay in a loose double ring outside the main outer ring of tall stones, but many of these had been moved to make way for their larger companions and their erecting tackle.

The whole construction was surrounded at some distance by a very ancient ditch and earth bank which reminded Avilla of Herik's very similar construction. Sonlith explained that that was all there was of the place in ancient times.

'But it was a beginning,' he said.

As he said this it began to snow again and this time it was heavier, so they made their way back to the large hut where they were brought food. For some time the pair sat in companiable silence enjoying their separate thoughts and the day had already given Avilla much to think about.

Their contemplation was shattered by the abrupt entry of one of the two of Herik's men. He wasted no time on preliminaries.

'Good, they said I would find you here, I have something of importance to tell you. We have seen a man here who we both last saw with Bork's troop.'

'Are you sure?' Asked Sonlith.

'We are certain,' replied the man. 'We both recognised him independently - he is here to spy and will surely leave soon taking his information back to Bork.' He looked troubled.

'Please join us - we must keep this to ourselves. Agreed?' Sonlith demanded.

They agreed.

'I suggest we let him overhear a conversation detailing some false information, perhaps exaggerating our military strength and our preparedness. My guess is that he will then leave in a hurry to report back to Bork.' Sonlith grinned. 'What Bork will make of the story I can only guess, but if it only gives him a few sleepless nights it will help.'

They decided the details and the man left to find his companion and then set the trap. Later that evening he returned to report success, the spy had swallowed the bait and had since left on foot heading North.

It was an eventful day.

They were not left alone long before a woman entered and after a brief nod to Sonlith

Turned to Avilla and said, 'Your hut is now ready for you, just call for Elln and he will show you.' And with that she was gone.

Avilla turned to Sonlith in surprise.

'You knew I would stay,' he said.

'Yes, at least I guessed,' replied Sonlith, 'but if you do stay I have a job for you. Everyone here has to earn their keep, and I'm afraid that even includes you.'

Avilla waited, wondering just what kind of a job it could be.

He could never have imagined in his wildest dreams the responsibility that Sonlith was about to place on his shoulders.

'The old one you met when you arrived is my second in command and is also my deputy. He is finding his responsibilities are getting too much for him and wishes to hand over to someone else.'

Avilla had no idea as to what was coming.

'I want you to take his place, I want you to be my deputy,' said Sonlith simply.

Avilla was speechless, his mind in a whirl.

'You can't be serious,' was all he could find to say.

'I am completely serious, I have followed your history since your birth was sung by the story singers, and I know you as well as you know yourself. You have all the right attributes of integrity and honesty. You believe in what we are doing here. But above all you are already known here for your deeds and you are highly respected by our people. - just ask anyone here.'

Avilla stared at Sonlith in disbelief.

'But I know nothing of your needs, ambitions, the protocol - In fact I am completely unfamiliar with what might be asked of me. A job yes, but I fear this responsibility is beyond my abilities.'

'Your unfamiliarity is just the asset I need. A fresh unbiased mind will bring a clear and fresh outlook to our situation and possible problems. A prime example is dealing with Bork.

'We will take it one step at a time. Firstly you will have to be elected by the council of course, all that rigmarole I shall explain to you in good time.'

'There is no need to decide now, and you will need to acquaint yourself with our responsibilities first, and then if you agree to serve you will be asked to give a speech of introduction to the council members. But for now please just say you will consider it. - You will honour me, I assure you.'

All Avilla could think of to say was, 'Er.....yes......er, thank you. I will give it much serious consideration.'

At this Sonlith called Elln and bid Avilla a peaceful night.

Avilla slept but little in the tiny but very comfortable one person hut that Elln showed him to, and before he turned in he got another shock.

'I will bid you good night,' Elln said, 'And I hope you will take the job, as do all my friends.'

Avilla felt that he should have known, there were few secrets in such a tightly organised community. Somehow this made him feel better.

****

To his surprise when they met the next morning Sonlith made no reference to his request, instead he said he was going to show Avilla the rest of the area and explain how their new and complex system was intended to work.

The snow held off and the night frost had frozen the thin layer into a sparkling blanket which lent an air of relaxed pleasure to their conversation. The bright sun created long shadows and the huge stones now draped in white seemed to Avilla to be smaller than he remembered but no less impressive.

They made their way away from the shadow of the stone circle to a wide flat plain. Nothing grew on it. The snow was smooth and uninterrupted by either shrub or tree.

Sonlith explained that this area was divided into 'fields'. Each field was the responsibility of one household and had been levelled, had its surface 'broken', and then 'planted' with seed from last season's crop. He demonstrated what these unfamiliar terms meant as he came to them.

An amazed and intrigued Avilla decided to simply listen and absorb the information leaving his questions until Sonlith had finished.

But Sonlith was only just starting. He quickly led on to where a group of low huts sat at the edge of yet another area of open fields. In these huts lived a small herd of goats. Some were out in the sun and seemed to have no difficulty in breaking the surface to get at the grass growing beneath.

And there were more fields and more wonders.

'We don't rely entirely on what is produced here, we have several large herds of deer living in the forest beyond these fields, and then of course there are the boar which we still hunt. And then there are the fruit bearing trees we have planted as well as large areas of wild plants which we are trying to tame.

'The river is rich with fish, and we use rope to make traps in which to catch them.

'Our climate here is warmer and the winters shorter and more gentle, I am uncertain if these methods can be adopted father north - but one day someone will try and succeed,' he concluded.

On returning Avilla thanked him and wandered off alone, he had much to occupy him.

But no sooner was he on his own than Elln appeared at his side, saying nothing but simply keeping him company. Avilla began to realise this was Elln's way of letting him know he had at least one firm friend.

And a friend was just what Avilla needed.

CHAPTER 22

⟮ **RESPONSIBILITY** ⟯

*D*uring the next few days it snowed quite heavily on and off. Movement was generally restricted to essential trips only. Avilla found himself left very much alone with Elln constantly close by in case he needed anything.

But importantly and gratifyingly, he had a visit from each of the other council members who separately and in their own way made it clear to him that they supported his election as deputy to Sonlith.

The more he learned the happier he became about his decision to stay. But it was Elln who eventually caused him to make his mind up about Sonlith's offer.

'Just think,' he said, 'who else is there that Sonlith can rely upon completely? There's no one but you. You are needed.'

Next day Avilla asked Sonlith as to his responsibilities.

'Don't worry,' Sonlith replied, 'we will deal with that as we go along. Besides we might change them, we may need to. Let us keep the arrangement flexible. Agreed?'

Avilla agreed and took Sonlith's hands in his.

'I will do my utmost to support you,' he said.

'I know I trust you as no other,' responded Sonlith.

And so the deal was done.

****

Eventually the day approached for Avilla to address the Council, and Sonlith had left him to decide what to say. Strangely it was Elln again who crystallized Avilla's thoughts.

'They know all about you, your story has been sung many times - so just tell them what you intend if you are elected. They don't like long speeches so keep it short and from your heart,' he advised.

The meeting took place in the big hut. A warming fire glowed in the hearth. The council members were all present and seated in a rough half circle. As Avilla entered the hum of conversation petered out and he found himself facing a sea of weathered faces some of which he had by now come to know.

Only council members were present with one unusual exception, for there in the background and seated just behind Sonlith was the figure of Elln. He was grinning happily.

Avilla decided to remain standing and after a shallow bow to his audience, and as there was no need to introduce himself, he began.

'I have been asked by Sonlith to offer myself to serve with you as a member of the council. I understand that if elected I shall do so as deputy to your leader Sonlith.

'I regard this as the highest honour I could ever have hoped to achieve, and I thank you all for this opportunity to be part of this group.

'Therefore I accept the proposal subject of course to being elected.

'You should know that whether elected or not I wish to make this place my permanent home and to share with you this future of which so far I have had only a short experience.

'Thank you.

'Has anyone any questions?'

There was a general murmur, and finally one councillor struggled to his feet.

'On behalf of us all, thank you for your willingness to take on this work. Sonlith will have great need of you in the hard days ahead. - I have just one question but I think we would all like to ask it.' He said. 'Just what chance do we have against the army we understand is on its way with Bork at its head and dedicated to destroying us.'

This was the one question Avilla was hoping to avoid - so he side-stepped it.

'I have sent my adopted son Greth to gather a force of armed fighters to assist us, and we have time to prepare. Bork cannot be here before snow has departed. In the meantime we will need to make our plans with care. Like all men he has his weaknesses which we must, and will exploit .

'I will not hide from you the fact that we may have a serious battle on our hands, but I am certain that Bork's day and way of life is over.

'Done.

'Finished.

'What you have here is the future for all men.

'We must, and will, win.'

There was a long silence as they considered his words, then slowly they started to clap and then to cheer him.

Avilla felt guilty. Words were easy, but he had as yet no clear idea as to how to match them with actions.

The meeting broke up and the members left with many a one shaking Avilla's hand as they went.

When he was alone again with Sonlith and the ever present Elln, he had the ballot procedure explained to him. To his surprise the day for this to take place had already been decided.

****

On the day of the vote, the area in and immediately around the great stones was cleared of snow and a rope strung round the perimeter where a trusted member of the group was posted at intervals to keep all but council members out. In the inner court two wooden tables had been set, one of which was labelled as approval of Avilla's election, whilst the other was marked for his rejection. These tables were set some distance apart. One person not a council member was stationed at the entrance to ensure that each councillor visited one and only one of the two tables.

At the entrance to the inner court was set a third table on which was a small pile of round black pebbles - one for each council member. This table was closely watched by council members and others.

A warming sun climbed towards it zenith as the people and the councillors started to arrive. Avilla stood watching with very mixed emotions as Sonlith waved his hand for the proceedings to begin.

One by one the councillors collected a black pebble and carried it into the inner chamber where he placed it on one of the two marked tables, then turned and left, his voting having been completed. Those outside could not see which table had been visited, nor could they know which table was which.

The last to perform this routine was Sonlith who collected the last stone on the table and walked calmly into the inner place. When he re-appeared he invited all the councillors plus Avilla to the inner sanctuary where the stones on each of the two inner tables were to be set against one another so that the table carrying those that were left decided the issue. However there was no need for this complication as there were no stones on the `rejection' table, they were all on the `approval' one. Avilla's acceptance to the council as Sonlith's deputy was unanimous.

There was a heartfelt cheer from the observers.

Avilla simply hoped that he would not let these good people down. More than that he was beginning to see that this really was a battle for the future - a battle they must win.

He left the great stones with many a friendly pat on the back and with a joyous Elln jumping and leaping at his side. Unbeknownst to Avilla, Elln had been actively canvassing behind his back, with obvious success.

Now Avilla started to have doubts as to their ability to withstand the hideous force that would be heading their way once the snow had gone. He needed space to think and to construct a strategy that stood a chance of succeeding. A strategy which had to be believable, a strategy that had to work.

He headed for his hut and with Elln letting in only those who could be constructive he put himself to think.

Again it was Elln who, several days later, triggered what Avilla considered might prove to be the most effective defence.

'I like your idea of using Bork's weaknesses against him,' the lad said naively whilst they were enjoying a simple lunch.

'That's it!' Avilla almost jumped for joy. But then more soberly - 'But will it work?'

He sat thinking for a good while, then quietly to himself. 'It has to, without a huge army we have nothing else.'

And so, slowly at first they began to plan.

It was a plan that relied heavily on Bork's and his troop's superstitious belief in the foul magic and the dreaded power he knew to be invested in these great stone circles, and here there was the biggest and the most powerful of them all. Power, he believed that if left unchecked would destroy his world.

Could Bork's own convictions be used against him?

It was a desperate ploy, but they had to try.

They had little else.

****

The only one who knew with absolute certainty the plan would work was young Elln. He had complete faith in Avilla, a faith which Avilla found disconcerting and misplaced. It nevertheless warmed his heart on these cold winter's days.

Life, even here was far from easy. Following a visit from a sole trader in bronze tools from the east there was an outbreak of severe colds and two families lost small infants, and an elderly man died whilst many were laid low for several days.

Towards the end of winter as green shoots began to appear on the trees, stocks of food ran low and many a stomach went empty.

But eventually the warmer weather began to arrive and hunting and fishing soon made up the deficiencies, and glum faces started to smile.

Of Avilla's adopted son, Greth, there was still no sign and they began to worry for him.

Then they had a visit from story singers who had come all the way from the far North.

They had news for Avilla that was to shake him to his very core, and even make him wonder about his decision to stay.

CHAPTER 23

❈ NEWS ❈

Although it was still mid-winter Avilla awoke early to feel the comforting rays of a sun now high in the sky. Tired of trying to find a way to defend themselves against the overwhelming force he knew would arrive as soon as weather would permit, he had slept until quite late. He was in fact just in time to share in the clan's mid-day meal taken on this exceptionally balmy day in the open.

As usual he found Elln by his side discretely pretending to be minding his own business whilst alert to any need Avilla may have.

The buzz of conversation was mostly concerned with the unusually mild weather and if it would last sufficiently to allow work on the great stone circle to re-start.

When Sonlith spoke they all listened.

'We will leave that work for a while yet,' he said, 'the ground is still very wet and the place would soon be churned to mud, and that would prevent any real progress for too long. Meanwhile we have other preparations to consider. I shall say more about these in due course. So all I ask is that you enjoy and make the most of today's marvellous sunshine.'

At this announcement there was a gentle cheer, and people drifted off to conduct their own activities.

Left alone Sonlith, Avilla, and of course the ever present Elln, sat quietly deep in their own thoughts for some time. Eventually Avilla began to speak, slowly and without conviction at first but then more confidently as he aired his thoughts on Bork's army and their own vulnerability for the first time.

The other two listened fascinated, and it has to be admitted, horrified.

'Bork is strong, determined, and has the largest and best trained armed force ever assembled,' he paused.

'He and his supporters are dedicated to destroying what we have here. He wants to wipe it out leaving no trace. And he is completely capable of doing it.'

His listeners looked grim, said nothing, but nodded in agreement.

'Further we can be sure that he will have trained his force well and they will obey him.'

No one spoke as the seriousness of the words sank home.

'Against this we have no adequate defence. Just a few stalwart men with crude arms and no training in battle tactics, and, we have to face it - with untested courage in the face of such overwhelming odds.

'Greth has failed to arrive, and worse we have heard nothing of him for some time. So cannot rely on him to be here to help us.

'Therefore, I am afraid that in a straight fight we will lose. And not just this place but our lives and those of our loved ones. From Bork we can expect little mercy'

They sat with grim faces.

Eventually Avilla began again.

'But one thing is certain my good friends, and I know you will agree - we dare not and will not yield to this crude aggressor.'

'Agreed!' Said two voices as one. And Avilla felt a little better.

He began again.

'But we do have one overwhelmingly powerful asset that can be turned into a terrifying and fearsome weapon with careful preparation.'

His listeners both looked puzzled.

'We have our truly impressive great stone circle.'

Sonlith looked worried, but Elln with a younger and sharper mind began to guess what was coming and chuckled, only to be silenced by Sonlith with a look.

'I'm sorry but I don't see.....................?'

'Well! It all starts with what I know of Bork.

'Whilst he tells everyone that he is out to destroy magic and superstition, he nevertheless does so because he believes in them and he fears them and the evil he imagines to be in to our simple structures. He is especially fearful of our ceremonies which to him are no more than cleverly woven spells.

'- All this,' he waved his arm around, 'would be the very source of his deep dread.'

A look of understanding appeared on Sonlith's weather beaten face.

'I begin to understand,' he said.

'I also believe that he has imbued his men with that same terrible fear as a means to get them to do battle. And a battle against us is a battle against the forces of evil.

'I have heard him use these very words.

'Now - Having seen your works here I can tell you that we can act the part of believers in evil and with the help of these great stones give a perfect show of magical chanting that would be enough to frighten even the most courageous to their death.

'I am certain that this will deter many of his troop from fighting by sheer fear of magical reprisals, and will weaken the resolve of the rest. And even if it doesn't stop the battle it will give us the edge we will surely need.'

Avilla knew that this plan was based on sand, but it was probably the best they could achieve. So was Sonlith convinced? Whichever way Avilla had made his pitch.

They sat for a long time in silence. Sonlith was not going to say yes without serious consideration. After all, the ultimate responsibility was his.

'Will it work?' he said so quietly it was almost to himself. Then in a normal voice -

'Yes, we will do it.'

Elln gave a whoop for joy, he at least was certain that it would succeed - Avilla had said so.

Their discourse ended there - as a forward scout ran up to say a pair of story singers looking very worse for wear had been spotted travelling very fast and were on their way in.

'They may have important news,' said Sonlith, 'But make sure they are fed and rested before they sing.'

The scout nodded and ran off to do his bidding.

****

It was early afternoon when the singers now somewhat refreshed sat quietly surveying the vast throng surrounding them. This was the biggest audience they had ever faced, and apart from the sentries and the very young everyone was there, which clearly indicated the importance the people placed on what the singers had to convey.

The sun hung as a great red orb drenching the great stones with blood. Even the wind held its breath.

An expectant silence enveloped the place.

Without further ado, and with a single brief nod of thanks to Sonlith they began.

`First an introduction,' the tallest of the two began, `although many of you will know us from previous visits.

`I am Yorg and my companion here is Pladge and we have travelled all the way from Avilla and Bork's clan in the distant North. Our first song therefore is of a member of this clan.'

And taking alternate verses Yorg then began -

`We will tell a tale of news both good and bad,
Of a life begun,
And a life at an end,
Of a glad event and one that's sad.

When Avilla left to travel south,
There was a thing he could not know,
His woman Chine was with child,
That it was his there was no doubt.'

At this everyone turned to gaze at Avilla who looked stunned.

`The child was born a healthy son.

Big and strong,
Fit and sound.
They named him well they named him Bron.'

As the news sank in Avilla began to grin, but his pleasure was short lived as Pladge continued -

'But the tribe was struck by the coughing disease.
And many there were who took to their cot,
Fair Chine caught that dreaded plague,
But her very life the thing did seize.'

Avilla could not disguise his pain, and the listeners sat in a respectful silence for a long time; until, in fact, Avilla nodded to the singers to continue.

'The once strong and active clan is now without a leader.
Bork has taken all the men.
Only women round the hearth,
They all want one thing - the quick return of Avilla.'

At this the singers stopped for rest and sustenance. Avilla with a supreme effort stayed to face people and friends grim with sympathy. He felt the loss of Chine deeply and he tried to concentrate on the knowledge that he had a natural son. He hoped that the boy would have something of his mother in him.

As to his return he could not cotemplate this until after he had faced up to Bork.

Now more relaxed the singers began again, and they had the attention of every ear present. This time it was just Yorg with the verses and Pladge rendering a kind of chorus in between.

> `We then went south
> On Bork's trail,
> And found his camp
> Hard by the river.
> And stuck they were
> By winter weather.
>
> Bork's vast army marching south,
> His progress passed by word of mouth.
>
> When he learned of his mother's child,
> He raged and stormed,
> And swore and cursed.
> Avilla he said must be killed
> His heart with the bile of hate is filled.
> Bork's great army is headed here,
> The day of warfare is drawing near.'

The story singers then eased the tension they had created with a couple of songs of a lighter note. One very popular one which the were asked to sing again described how Lit pill invented the sledge and finished up in the river. Most of the young lads present began to wish they had been there. Lamentably their were no suitable slopes here.

After sunset Sonlith took Avilla and Elln with the story singers to the big hut where they could interrogate them in private. What they learned was both good and bad.

'Bork's two spies returned whilst we were there and Bork guessed they had been fed exaggerated information, but it worried him since they had been found out and so easily duped. 'The men were left in no doubt about Bork's poor opinion of them,' Pladge reported.

'We also believe that not everyone is happy with Bork's aims. But although we tried people were afraid to speak out so it must remain a suspicion - but a very strong one. And we don't know who or how many there are who think like this.'

'Do you know when he will march?' Asked Avilla.

'No. But he will not set out until the snow has truly gone,' replied Yorg.

'Which implies his arrival at or about mid-year's day,' mused Sonlith almost to himself.

'We thank you for this knowledge. Tell me what are your plans now?' He asked.

The singers glanced at one another, and Yorg took a deep breath and said it all in one go -

'Well whatever the outcome, the forthcoming meeting between yourselves and Bork will determine the future of the two Realms for the foreseeable future, and as such should be set in song. We were therefore hoping that you would allow us to stay here to be on hand for whenever it takes place.'

Sonlith looked at Avilla who nodded his approval.

'Stay and be welcome,' he said.

'Thank you,' Yorg said humbly.

But before then many more story singers arrived determined to carry the news of such an important event to all corners of the Realms.

At this the discussion broke up and Avilla, after a sympathetic pat on the back from Sonlith and a sqeeze of his hand from Elln, retired to mourn for the loss of his lovely brave Chine. He would try to find his new son but that would have to be later - if he survived.

CHAPTER 24

⸎ **PREPARATIONS** ⸎

At first it seemed that there was little that could be done by way of preparation for Bork's army, but there was, and it kept the whole group busy throughout the winter, which turned out to be unusually mild.

The first thing Sonlith did was to organise a meeting of the whole body of those who would be present when the troops arrived - including visitors. Only the very young were excluded.

He was lucky as the weather was perfect, one could almost believe that summer had begun. The recent snow had melted and the sun's rays warmed the wide space close by as Sonlith strode out to confront his people feeling less confident than he tried to look.

Well aware of the seriousness of the occasion the noise of conversation ceased almost immediately Sonlith raised his hand.

'Firstly,' he began without preamble, 'everything you hear at this get-together is very, very secret.'

He stopped to let this sink in.

'If any of this gets back to Bork it could cost us our very lives.'

He stopped again.

'Now in regard to this security, if any of you see someone you don't recognise in our midst - you must tell me or Avilla here immediately. It may be someone taking knowledge of our preparations to our enemy.

'Secondly, be in no doubt Bork has one thing and one thing only on his mind and that is to wipe us out, and he has travelled a long, long way to achieve this, and is determined to succeed.'

Sonlith gazed down on a sea of worried and frightened faces, so he set about restoring confidence.

'However we do have plans, and we intend to survive this evil onslaught, and I shall be talking separately to those of you who will be involved in each part of the scheme. However, there is one thing of massive importance in which you must all take part. It is possible that Bork may trap us in a siege. Should this happen every morsel of food and every drop of water will be needed - so please start now gathering and storing whatever you can and hide it. It might save a life.

'This is the last time I will talk to you all like this, so please come to either of us if you have a problem. Try and remember that we are the defenders here, and as such we have right on our side. Thank you.'

He did not ask for questions and turned and left the arena to call the council members to the first of many councils of war.

****

All the council members were present in the big hut and before the addressed them Sonlith asked Elln to stroll about outside to discourage any would be eavesdroppers. Elln grinned and dashed off to do his bidding.

When he had gone Sonlith asked Avilla to explain what he had in mind to enhance the aura of mystery and power associated with the great stones.

'I will outline my ideas for your consideration, but I am only too pleased to welcome any you may dream up. Remember the idea is to play on their superstition so much so that they will want to turn and run, although I think this to be most unlikely, but we may succeed in weakening their resolve.

'Should this strategy fail we will arm and train our men folk to be ready to fight.'

And so after much discussion several plans were established with volunteers from the councillors to put them in place.

Confidence began to replace hopelessness as the session continued.

'At least they would be actively doing something positive instead of simply waiting for the inevitable.' Sonlith pointed out to Avilla as they broke up eager to put the plans in place.

A pair of scouts were sent north to give at least one day's warning of Bork's arrival with strict instructions not to be seen.

A second pair was sent east to attempt to locate Greth and his possible troop with instructions to hurry them up if possible, and to return speedily if Greth was delayed in any way.

Soon every able bodied person was furiously busy and the place began to resemble the hive of activity it was at the height of the summer. Even when the weather kept people under cover plans continued to be eagerly discussed with many a good idea being thought up and acted upon.

Avilla was amazed to see the atmosphere of aggressive confidence that now invaded the whole place. But in his quieter moments, alone with his thoughts, his doubts drifted to the surface, and a deep fear clutched his heart.

He knew what Bork was capable of.

****

Before long all that could be done had been done. All preparations were complete. None of the four scouts had as yet returned, and Sonlith began to be worried that the normal activities that usually took place in the early days of summer were behind schedule. The ground had not yet been prepared for seed. Urgent repairs to buildings had not been carried out. Work on erecting the big stones had all but stopped.

He called another clan meeting where he gave priority to maintaining their preparations to receive Bork but emphasised the need to transfer any spare effort to normal work.

The snow went, the ground dried, and work on the next big stone re-started.

Days grew longer and Avilla joined a group whose task it was to prepare the ground for seed.

At first he found the work hard not being used to a full day of physical work, but his muscles quickly hardened and his stamina improved and with this came a real sense of creation. He even found that he could ignore the ache from the wounds he received in his fight with Tallon in what seemed like a lifetime ago. Sadness at the loss of Chine eased, but never left him.

He felt for the first time in his life that he was genuinely building for the future. There was the sense of adding something to the earth instead of merely taking from it.

Avilla had now proved for himself that his feelings that this way of life was better, more satisfying, and more creative was right. It appealed to some instinct buried deep in his very core. He was at one with it.

It then came to him that he must set about learning all he could and if they survived Bork he would return north teaching the new way. He would bring his natural son up to continue this work.

Then it came to him that for the first time for a long time he was contented.

This was noted by Sonlith and especially by Elln who took the opportunity of Avilla's relaxation to pull his leg.

'You have spent so much time breaking the earth you are beginning to crumble yourself,' he ventured one day. And to his surprise instead of the usual friendly cuff of his ear Avilla laughed so much his sides ached and an amazed crowd gathered round wanting to know what had amused him. They were not impressed when he simply said 'I'm just happy.'

****

Sonlith however, with the responsibility resting on his shoulders, took matters more seriously and called regular council meetings to review progress and set priorities. To his surprise things went well and soon he too began to relax.

He even arranged a morale lifting evening round the fire and invited the story singers to entertain them on the clear understanding that there were to be no serious songs. This they did and it was no surprise that the now notorious Lit pill featured often. Avilla suspected that at least some of the stories were exaggerated.

>'On a hot and sweaty summer's day,
> Lit pill wanted to find a cooler way
> Of being. - Cheers from the listeners.
> He tied a long rope to a high tree fair
> And swung on the end of it through the air.
> Far and wide. - Laughter.
> Over the river even for him was rash,
> He entered the water with a great splash.
> - Cheers and laughter.
> Disappeared. - Ooooo.
> Drng's tame wolf jumped in too,
> Grabbed our Lit pill by his shoe - Laughter.
> And dragged him out. - Cheers.
> But Lit pill was no fool
> For now he was extremely cool. - Laughter.
> And wet.' - Much laughter and cheers.

The evening was enjoyed by all, which was as well since the following day the scouts from the north arrived to be followed shortly after by the two from the east.

Sonlith and Avilla took them aside to hear what they had to report.

Tired scouts gave their messages briefly and to the point.

Bork, they said was well on his way. He had a very big army. It took them a very long time to pass with Bork at its head riding on the back of a horse. The speaker held up both hands with fingers extended several times.

They estimated he would arrive in just a few days and held up one hand with fingers extended.

Sonlith and Avilla heard the report in silence and thanked the scouts. And having sworn them to secrecy dismissed them.

Things began to look bad.

And were soon to get worse.

The scouts from the east reported that they had found Greth and that he had collected just a small group of men, they held up two hands. These men were poorly equipped and were making slow progress due to a lack of discipline. They could not tell how long they would take to arrive, but they had met with Greth and advised him as to the absolute urgency.

Again, the scouts were schooled to silence, and thanked.

Sonlith and Avilla regarded each other grimly.

`Well it looks as if we will be dependent on your strategy with the stones if we are to survive,' said Sonlith.

Avilla nodded, said nothing and tried to look confident.

The next few days were spent with everyone busy putting the plan into effect.

It seemed a desperate gamble.

CHAPTER 25

❧ BORK CONTINUES HIS MARCH SOUTH ❧

*A*s he rode astride his horse 'Flame' at the head of his formidable army, Bork's confidence was high. He knew from his scouts that there was now no opposition between him and his goal that could delay him, let alone stop him.

The weather had turned warm and it was dry underfoot. Trail and tracks here in the Southern Realm of Kingdoms were well used and easy to march on, and they made good progress. They were still mostly surrounded by woodland but the deserted groups of houses they came across and used as temporary camps were surrounded by broad areas of grassy flattened land whose purpose was much debated by the troops. The predominant view was that the ground had been cleared simply to make it easier to move things and people about.

The truth, that these were areas set out for cultivation of crops, an unfamiliar concept to these people from the north, and was not even guessed at.

They did not however, have it all their own way and suffered quite a few serious casualties.

Displaced tribes hiding in the woods made frequent and often devastating raids on Bork's army as it passed through the more densely packed trees. Using both slings and throwing spears they would hide in waiting, fling all they had in one salvo and run off dispersing as they went.

Bork lost several men with serious wounds without catching a single one of the perpetrators. In this unfamiliar environment his scouts were proving useless.

Tempers became frayed as Bork blamed his men, threatening them with severe punishment. And the anti Bork faction silently grew.

In all this it was noted that the women, who brought up the rear were not attacked. When he realised this Bork had the women march dispersed within the main group. This did reduce the casualties but slowed them down as the men naturally gave most of their attention to the ladies, and his troop became strung out over a considerable distance making them additionally vulnerable.

****

It was now well into the summer and daily the sun rose higher in the sky. As they progressed southwards the track became a road, the sheltering trees sparser, and the daily temperature much hotter. Rest stops became more frequent, and the march significantly slower.

Bork fairly accurately guessed that they would arrive at the great circle at about mid-summer. He realised this without knowing its significance.

Then two events took place within days of each other, one bad the other one good.

It was during one of the overnight camps that Drng came to Bork with a strange problem. He claimed that a number of familiar faces were no longer present and he thought a number of the troops had absconded.

At first he was not believed, but Bork lined the men up to check and it became obvious that the army had shrunk. When questioned the men admitted that some of their comrades had decided that they would return to their home clans. Their reasons were varied and very human.

A couple had been quite seriously hurt, a few were missing their families, and some had come a long way and were just home sick.

It was a set back for Bork, but Drng persuaded him that they were better without men whose hearts were not in the battle. To improve moral Bork decided on a rallying speech, called all the men together and seated astride his horse to hide his short stature he proceeded to address them.

'Men - comrades in arms, friends.

'We have come a very long way, and in doing so we have overcome many difficulties. In this you have proved yourselves to be loyal, strong, and a credit to yourselves. Never before has such a march been attempted by so grand an army. Our journey will make history and will be sung about by the story singers for ever.

'We are very near our goal and our victory of which I am certain will make heroes of every single one of us. You will be celebrated on your return home, when you will be rich from the spoils.

'As to the fight, my spies have convinced me that there is only a small armed force reigned against us, and I fully expect that when they realise how strong we are they will quickly surrender, leaving the place and its contents for us to plunder at our leisure.

'In fact I intend to offer them surrender terms which they will have little choice but to accept, their only alternative being to fight and be destroyed.

'It is a great task we have undertaken. The future of life as our ancestors have led it for countless generations is at stake.

'This is a goal of historic importance, and it is down to us, no one else can attempt it, we and we alone hold all we believe in, in our hands.

'We must not fail.

'We dare not fail.'

He had spoken from the heart and his passion and his sincerity were obvious. But he was surprised when after a pause his speech was greeted by loud and prolonged cheering.

They were on his side to a man.

He thought they would go through fire for him, and his confidence was restored.

A couple of days later the second event occurred.

The advanced scouts returned to report that a large number of huts sat in a clearing ahead of them, and unusually the clan members were all at home. Also it was clear that they knew of Bork's approach and were preparing a feast for them.

Suspecting a trap Bork approached with caution but relaxed as their chief came forward and welcomed him.

The chief told Bork that they of all the local clans supported what Bork was about. They were in fact in a constant state of conflict with the people of the great stone circle, and there were constant skirmishes for the ownership of land.

The army took advantage of this friendly clan and stayed for some time.

But there was a further surprise for Bork.

As they were about to leave a smart troop of armed and disciplined men marched forth, presented themselves to Bork and asked formally to join his army and fight under his command.

This group more than made up for their recent losses and everyone was delighted.

****

Now only a few days out, confident and eager, they sang as they marched unchallenged to the final confrontation.

An unstoppable force was about to descend on Sonlith and his peaceful clan.

CHAPTER 26

❧ **BORK ARRIVES** ❧

The moment that Avilla had been dreading had arrived. A scout returned and reported to Sonlith that Bork was just a single day's march away. He also spoke of the huge size of the army.

'More men than I have ever seen at one time,' he said.

Bork well aware of the disastrous effect of first sight of the great stones might have on his army decided to camp a short distance away where they were hidden from view. He only had supplies for a few days so he knew he had to act decisively and soon. He used this time to prepare the troops with formal assemblies where equipment was checked and each man addressed by Bork in person.

When they were stood to on parade his army presented a truly formidable force. Bork was well aware of the scouts sent out by Sonlith but ignored them, thus allowing them to report back with the grim truth that they had witnessed.

Bork decided that he must have a good fine day for his attack, and was assured by his weather prophet that it would be good for the next several days.

The day before his intended aggression Bork sent an envoy in to arrange a meeting between himself, accompanied by Drng, and Sonlith with his second in command. He warned the envoy to speak to no one of what he had seen of the enemy when he returned, on the pain of death if he did.

The meeting was arranged. Sonlith would meet Bork in no-man's land between the camp and the stone circle. Sentries from both sides were posted to keep eavesdroppers away.

Sonlith and Avilla were the first to arrive at the neat grassy clearing in the trees. It was warm, and strong midday sunlight filtered through the leaves dappling the ground. They each chose a fallen log on which to sit. They did not have to wait long before Bork impressive on horseback with Drng by his side strode out from the shelter of the trees to stop just in front of the other pair.

Sonlith and his companion remained seated to indicate a total lack of respect.

Now it had been a long time since Bork had clapped eyes on Avilla and for a long moment he failed to recognise him, when he did it was a terrible shock. The one person he hated most in this life and had sworn to kill was there seated boldly in front of him now as the great circle chief's second in command. Of this he had had no warning and it threw him off balance his mind in a turmoil, his heart in a rage.

'You!' Bork yelled, 'I will see you dead before I leave here,' he shouted.

Avilla's reply was to point out calmly that they couldn't hear him whilst he sat up there on his silly animal.

Bork in a fury had no choice but to dismount, which he managed only with some difficulty to the obvious amusement of the others.

Drng nodded his recognition of Avilla who returned his greeting.

They waited for Bork to recover. Then into the silence that followed Sonlith spoke with a quiet calm.

'I am Sonlith, chief of these people by nomination,' he said, 'and I presume you are Bork, self appointed chief, and your companion here is Drng.

'Now I presume you have called us here for some purpose so I suggest that you get on with what you have to say as we have constructive work to get on with, unlike you whose only ambition is to wage war on innocent people and destroy them, their places, and their way of life.'

Bork was not used to being spoken to with such a lack of deference and it disturbed him.

He drew a deep breath and in a stern voice began -

'In return for sparing your lives I have come to offer you the opportunity to surrender. You will be required to dismantle your great stone circle and to acknowledge me as the sole ruler of the Southern Realm of Kingdoms.'

Sonlith threw back his head and roared with genuine laughter.

'You simple fool. If we did give in to you how long do you think your rule would last? Neither you nor anyone else can stop the changes which we are involved in. The new ways will offer people a better life and whatever you do now will soon be overtaken by the inevitable. Neither you nor anyone else can stop ideas. Here we call it progress.

'We will not surrender.'

Bork snorted and rejected this statement with a scornfull grunt, but Drng simply sat looking thoughtful, he thought that there was a formidable truth in Sonlith's words. They were not merely a boast.

'Then you have brought this on yourselves. I intend to smash you and all you stand for. I will teach you a lesson which others will take as a warning to reject your ways.'

He shouted this, leaped onto his horse and without waiting for Drng galloped headlong into the trees.

When Bork had disappeared Drng slowly stood, strode across to Sonlith and Avilla, shook the hand of each in turn and walked slowly and thoughtfully away without a word.

Sonlith looked questioningly at Avilla who shrugged his shoulders and looked puzzled. Clearly they did not know what to make of Drng's extraordinary action.

'Well, that would seem to be that. I think we had better prepare for a visit from ruler Bork and his army,' Sonlith said ruefully.

'Yes.' Avilla replied simply.

As they strode through the lovely peaceful glades both men turned their thoughts to what they had agreed had to be done to prepare for what must now be an inevitable onslaught.

Whilst back in Bork's camp his men were wondering why there was this delay. They knew what was to be done and simply wanted to get on with it. But they had no idea as to the shocking effect sight of the great stone circle was to have.

****

Later that day Bork, together with Drng and a guide crept to within sight of the great stones. The effect on both men was profound and quite different.

In Bork's case he had never imagined anything so huge, the stones seemed to reach up to touch the very sky. He had difficulty believing that this was the work of man. He half believed that these things could not be achieved without supernatural help. In this he was convinced that it was magic, an evil magic no less and therefore his war to destroy it was justified. But what it all meant or what it was for he had little idea, any attempt to discover its meaning he had ruthlessly rejected. He was a man convinced and he was glad. His struggle to get here with an army would, he felt, have been worthwhile. History would no doubt claim him as a hero.

He even thought that the object of his lust, the lively Noon, would be unable to resist him, and his face broke into a grin of sheer anticipation.

He would move his troop into position this very night and attack at dawn the following day. With this decision made he was overwhelmed by a great sense of peace.

Drng on the other hand was equally impressed by the sight of what he saw, but its impact on him was very different. His admiration for what Sonlith had achieved was paramount, and he wondered what other wonders lay there, and was afraid that they would be wilfully destroyed without his ever having knowledge of them. He felt an overwhelming shame of what they were about to do. As they crept away his heart became angry at Bork and all he stood for. But as Bork told him of his decision he realised it was too late to change events.

CHAPTER 27

⚔ **NIGHT-TIME** ⚔

*I*t was fortunate for both sides that the night following the meeting between the chiefs was a moonless one.

As the sun began to set Sonlith and Avilla were busy with final arrangements when a scout ran headlong onto their hut with the news that the army was on the move and heading towards them, and would be in place for a dawn attack the next day.

Avilla grinned at Sonlith, the timing could not have been better, tomorrow would be mid summer day and they would start with their grand dawn celebrations only this time they would be very special.

They called the council, told them the news and set them to complete the arrangements, but only after dark, and quietly so as to maintain secrecy.

Later a second runner arrived having had to indulge in some tricky manoeuvring to avoid Bork's troops who were, he said, moving into position, and he was able to give Sonlith a good idea as to their disposition. But his real message was that he had just come from Greth who unfortunately was still two days away.

Some distance from the stone circle a loose camp had sprung up from which laughter and occasional singing could be heard. Story singers aware that history was in the making had arrived from all over the country anxious not to miss recording it in song. Word had got round and here they all were to witness whatever took place.

Bork had no time to think he was busy directing his force.

He had carefully considered what he must do and now he was laying the foundations of his attack.

There was little point in attacking the huts lying some distance from the great stone circle. They were probably deserted anyway and his army would be too widely spread out and difficult to control. So he had decided on a simple direct attack on the stone circle itself. If he captured it, he argued, he would be in charge of the very heart of the enemy, the battle would effectively be over. Also it was a single large and obvious target.

He divided his men into three groups, two of which would perform an armed charge roughly from the northeast and driving directly into the open end of the inner circle, one from the left the other from the right. He would head one of these armed thrusts, and Drng would head the other. If he attacked at dawn and the day should be cloudless, as anticipated, then the sun would be directly in the eyes of any would-be defenders, who would present perfectly lit targets for his men. The third group, the largest, was to spread out around the back of the stones and some little distance from the surrounding ditch, Their task was to prevent any retreating enemy escaping. A second task of this troop was to hold any opposition forces which might be tempted to re-group and counter attack.

As he moved his men into position he made sure that they were just out of sight of the ring of stones so as not to be detected by the opposition, but also so they would not be discouraged by the sight of the great circle until the order to charge had been given, and there was no turning back.

When he had satisfied himself that all were in position and ready for the fray, Bork reflected on his battle strategy. So far he could see only one drawback - he had no knowledge as to the number and disposition of Sonlith's men. However his scouts had identified only a small group of soldiers which they described as untrained and poorly equipped.

Having satisfied that all that could be done had been done, he strode over to where Drng was resting, head on a log. Their conversation was brief.

'Is everything done?' Bork asked.

'All that you have ordered.' Drng replied.

'Good, 'till tomorrow then.'

''Till tomorrow.'

With that Bork returned to his own troop, settled himself down and tried to sleep, but sleep wouldn't come.

Anger, doubts, memories, strategies, pain, and lust chased each other round his brain without logic and without ceasing.

At one point in a momentary lapse he decided to call the whole thing off, but a picture of Avilla looking thoroughly satisfied quickly chased the thought away.

Then, unasked, the thought of Drng filled his mind. Something, he could not decide what, had been troubling him increasingly about that young man. Something was not quite as it was. Some lack of eagerness in carrying out his tasks. Just something about the way he looked back when

Bork addressed him. Something was not right. And he determined to keep a watch on him.

As for Drng himself, he was wondering why he was obeying Bork. He had realised too late that he fundamentally disagreed with the objectives of this war. He liked what he had seen of Sonlith and had always respected Avilla and wished them no harm. Besides this he dearly wanted to know much more about their way of life, which seemed in all respects to be more appealing than the old ways.

Tomorrow was hard upon him what the blazes was he going to do?

This night was to prove to be a very long one for everyone involved.

And not the least for the ordinary people of Sonlith's group, aware of the proximity of an aggressive army without knowing what steps, if any, had been taken for their protection.

Avilla, Sonlith and their team which was composed of all the council members and a handful of helpers were still at work preparing the site. It was hard going and they would only just have finished in time for a short rest.

They also got no sleep that night.

CHAPTER 28

❧ BEFORE THE STORM ☙

*N*one of this intense human activity had any effect on the natural world around them.

As midnight approached the last of these busy people retired to their sleeping quarters, a distant wolf howled briefly and was answered by another quite close by.

A pair of owls called and were instantly challenged by another. A tiny waft of air breathed through the leaves of the surrounding woods causing them a gentle dance.

A mole broke the surface to sniff the night air, its nose doing the job of its poor eyesight and in doing so startled a hunting hedgehog.

Moths of all sizes flitted and darted, seldom settling for long in a desperate search for a partner. Insects of the night settled on leaves and flower heads to rest tired wings. Glow worms winked their greenish ghostly light in the undergrowth where the trees began.

A boar grunted as he awoke and left his warm den to begin his nightly foraging. Bats zigzagged in and out of the trees, greedy for insects. Nearby small mice chittered and another owl glided silently down, a pale ghost against the velvet dark. Somewhere far away an animal screamed either in pain or ecstasy. The sound of movement and of intensive life was everywhere.

High above bright stars winked down lending an aura of magic whilst silhouetting the giant stones.

But as yet none of this had anything to do with the world of man.

As for them -

Noon shed a tear for her murdered son and felt a thrill of hate for Bork run through her frame.

Lit pill thought of a new way to move large objects, glad to be left out of the conflict.

Fellysin thinking warmly of Drng hugged her knees, and hoped for his safety tomorrow.

Elln's young mind was a whirl of exciting anticipation, not without fear.

And a long way away Herik thought of Avilla and hoped he would prevail.

Even farther away Avilla's natural son dreamed unremembered dreams.

****

And the world uncaring, continued its steady turning, bringing the dawn and the future slowly but inevitably nearer.

CHAPTER 29

⋐ **PRE - DAWN** ⋑

It was still dark, when Bork slowly awakening from a brief but deep doze lay back and allowed the import of this day gradually to fill his mind and soul. On this day he would find his destiny. He was nearing the final act of his great struggle and he knew that success was in his grasp at last. He was about to change the future for ever. After today the old ways would be re-established and his ancestors would rejoice. He felt that his was the hand of destiny. He felt that he was about to effect an act of great heroism, he was destiny's child.

And he knew he would be victorious.

After all there would be little opposition to this the largest and best equipped army in both Realms. His men fully equipped and trained were in place, ready and eager to do his bidding. He believed from information provided by his scouts that standing against him was a small untrained and poorly armed group of men reluctant to fight and commanded by members of the their council inexperienced in the skills of war.

He was certain he would prevail and felt no sympathy for those he was about to subdue, after all they had refused, even laughed, at his offer of surrender terms. Whatever took place, even death - it would be on their heads.

He felt a glow of satisfaction as he contemplated the possible fate of his uncle Avilla, murderer of his father, and bitter rival, now it seemed appointed second in command to Sonlith, chief and leader of these self satisfied upstarts whom he was about to face. He pondered the problem - should he kill him and have done with him for ever, or would this create a martyr whose spirit would haunt the rest of his days? Or should he allow him his life and risk a future uprising? The bile rose in his throat as he pictured his enemy and rage gripped his belly, his hatred was absolute. This iniquitous pile of rubbish with his infamous beliefs stood for everything he detested. No, he decided - Avilla could not be allowed to live, he would make his death a priority. With this thought came swift satisfaction, and he settled back to contemplate the future in this quiet time before day broke and to dream of the prospect of glory that he knew lay just a very short time away.

He was glad that after a long and difficult journey his victory would be on mid-summer's day, a day considered auspicious by those opposing him, but to Bork just another day. It gave his mind extra relish. He was about to eliminate such superstition for ever. He would see to it that it would vanish from the minds of men.

Blood had been spilt on the way and it had been a tough slog, but it would soon all be worth it, and he and his followers would be immensely rich, and be rid of these conscience stricken fools. There were rumours of hordes of gold, which, if true would soon be discovered with the help of a little torture; and he had just the man for the job, Iaan Bad Breath truly enjoyed his work and had never failed.

With that his mind turned to the comely Noon and imagined her giving in to his greedy desires. If she refused him, he would force her and he savoured these familiar lascivious thoughts.

But all too soon his girl food taster entered his tent and offered him cold meat having first eaten some herself in case of poison, for now this would have to be enough, later he would fill his belly with the best of the victor's spoils.

Outside his men were preparing themselves for battle and the noise of their voices interspersed with occasional coarse laughter and the rattle of the equipment of battle, filtered dully through the thick animal skin wall of his tent. It gladdened and excited him.

He next called for his henchmen-bodyguards Terck and Sollin and with their help and encouragement he donned his thick leather chest armour, checking carefully that there were no gaps where a knife or spear blade might enter too easily.

Suddenly Bork's features grew red with anger and he waved his bodyguard closer. Hesitantly they obeyed him and cautiously moved closer, you never knew with Bork when angry. He spoke in a whisper so as not to be overheard by anyone listening immediately outside the tent.

'I have a mission for you both which you will now swear to me on your lives to do, and which you will carry out if I am wounded and unable to do it myself.'

Fearfully both men swore to do so, well aware of what would happen to them if they refused.

'Should Drng fail in battle and survive, you will take his woman Fellysin and kill her in full view of Drng.'

Both men blanched and tried to hide their surprise and distaste for this terrible order.

'You must swear,' said Bork, 'or I will deal with you now.' He emphasised the point by stroking the blade of his dagger.

They swore to do his bidding, and tried hard to disguise their feelings by busying themselves with preparing Bork for the fray, and hoped that they would never be called upon to carry out their promise.

At last, clothed and ready for battle, he dismissed the men with instructions to send Drng his second in command to him. Drng entered almost immediately and as the tent flap fell closed behind him stood waiting, his expression unreadable in the sombre flickering gloom of the oil lamps.

Now in this final showdown Bork had realised that he was no longer sure of Drng's loyalty, and was glad that he held captive the lovely Fellysin, Drng's great love, against his continued support. He smiled grimly as he reflected on the order he had just given his bodyguard who even now would be standing guard by his tent ready to defend him until death. But Bork also knew his men, and was certain that knowledge of his recent order would be secretly conveyed to Drng, in fact he was depending on it to keep Drng in line.

Drng stood politely and waited.

Bork drew himself up to his full height and grinned, he felt in control.

'Well this will be the last battle, and after there will be great spoils and I predict the men who have helped me to succeed will all be rich. We cannot fail and we will be seen as famous our names remembered with glory throughout the rest of time. This is a great deed we are about to perform.'

He looked questioningly into Drng's eyes but to his disappointment read nothing there.

'Tell me now that the men are ready?' It was an order not a question.

'Ready!' Drng's answer was prompt.

'And what about you?' Bork demanded.

'Ready!' He repeated.

'I want the first charge to succeed. I don't want to be chasing loose and armed enemy all over the field,' Bork said, 'is that understood?'

'Yes it is,' replied Drng.

'Remember on my order to charge you and your men will move immediately forward from one side as I and my men will move at the same time from the other.'

'Clear?'

'Clear,' said Drng. 'Will you be on horseback?'

'No,' said Bork, 'he's too valuable.'

Drng was thankful, as Flame had originally been his horse and he was anxious for the animal's safety. He had many times regretted handing him to Bork.

'Go now, and be ready for my order which I will call when the sun appears on the horizon,' then as an after thought, 'and may good fortune be with you.'

'Thank you - and with you,' Drng replied stiffly.

Bork waved his hand in a gesture of dismissal.

With a brief nod Drng turned on his heel and left the tent.

Once alone, Bork slung his trusty shield on his left arm, hefted his spear in his right hand, and left the tent eager to have this thing begin.

He found that outside it was still dark, and fresh from the oil lamp lighting, he at first could see little, but he was immediately aware of his men deployed as he had instructed just out of sight of the ring of great stones. As he emerged the army who had fought at his bidding during the long march South gave a scattered shout.

'Bork..........Bork.........Bork...............Victory for The Boar.'

He grew taller and stood straight to hide his shorter right leg, and facing his men he saluted them.

Then turning to face his enemy he gave the order for the men to move forward towards their objectives, and the whole of his army walked slowly towards the circle to take up their positions from which the attacking charge would be launched.

The sun had not yet risen but the stones could just be seen, massive, and darkly silhouetted as they were against the pale pre-dawn sky. The sight was awe-inspiring, even frightening enough. For his men nothing remotely like this had ever been seen before, and it proved to be beyond their imagination.

Staggered as they were that men could have constructed such a thing, their normally rational minds riddled with superstition were unable to exclude a terrible feeling of dread. Powerful magic was abroad this day, and these huge stones were its source. It is difficult to imagine the paralysing effect of this awesome sight on the men. All were affected by the terrible majesty of the scene and it caused shards of fear to stab into otherwise brave hearts. Panic was very close and only the greater fear of the consequences prevented them from running. But it was not just their first sight of the huge stones so carefully arranged that caused Bork's men to halt and waiver in their disbelief and shock, It was also what Sonlith and his people had prepared.

As the dawn began to lend colour to the scene they saw a sight never before witnessed.

The outer ditch had been filled to overflowing with large hawthorn branches creating a continuous barrier. Trees of Rowan resplendent with red fruit had been closely planted at intervals atop the encircling bank. But it was what had been done to the stones themselves that struck awe into the minds of the attackers. Each great stone was encircled twice by a thick pure white rope, and the same rope was looped between the stones and tied in the middle in a loose knot such that the ends reached nearly to the ground. The head of each stone and the connecting lintels were garlanded with crown of flowers of many colours which hung in great loops down the sides of each one.

In the middle of the central ring with its opening facing the dawn stood a pair lonely figures dressed in robes of purest white. They stood by a single table-like stone waiting quietly.

Outside the central group more men were to be seen, their white garments showing in the gaps between the great outer stones, its ring of stones as yet still far from complete.

Even the most courageous of Bork's men hesitated at the sight it all.

It was a truly awesome scene, and the army's forward movement came to an untidy halt and a sort of moan of confusion rose from the force.

Even Bork hesitated, this he had not anticipated and he needed time to decide what action to take. Another factor that puzzled him was that there was not a single armed defender in sight. It appeared that all they had to do was to walk in and declare the place captured, but was it a trap? He couldn't be sure.

Then Bork recognised that one of the two central figures was Avilla and the old hatred rose in his gorge. He determined that the detested believer in all this false magic would be the first to die and he Bork would finish him. He remembered with hate gripping his soul that this was the very Avilla, murderer, betrayer, dealer in superstition and sworn enemy, was the one who had killed his own brother, Bork's father.

As he struggled to control his anger another thought, unsought, forced itself to the front of his mind. He remembered Zapallor the soothsayer's prediction that his death would be "of his own making - but not by his own hand." The words seemed to contradict themselves and he was tired of puzzling over them, even Zapallor herself admitted under the threat of death that she could see in them no meaning. With a tremendous effort he thrust these thoughts from his mind - this was no time for doubts, his would be an easy victory sung about for ever by the story singers.

Glancing round he saw a sea of raised spears many with a small cloth flag fluttering jauntily in the light breeze with its crude effigy of a boar's head. Grim faces stared out from under a variety of leather helmets as his men stood armed and clad for battle.

He thought that in spite of the shock his men had experienced at the site of the stones and in spite of a dread feeling of the great power emanating from them, they were trained soldiers ready to go on his orders.

So, with this comforting thought Bork cast all doubt aside.

He had no choice - It was his destiny.

No more waiting.

He decided - it was time.

But before he could give the order and as his army ceased to cry out, into this unearthly quiet came a strange but melodious sound.

Low at first a slow chant of many voices in harmony rose and filling the air. It had a penetrating quality and seemed to come from the white garbed group at the centre of the stones. In waves of a hypnotic rhythm the chant gradually increased in volume. It seemed to be rooted in the earth so persistent was it. It rose and fell from many throats in waves of sound. Occasional words could be distinguished but the overall meaning whilst not understood seemed to be threatening.

For Bork's men it was as if a spell was being added to the to the already powerful forces ranged against them, and their resolve wavered. Fear began to grip them.

This they had not been warned about. This changed matters.

No one moved except the figure at the centre of the stones, Sonlith. The pale flame of an oil lamp flickered on the stone table in front of him and it was over this that Sonlith now passed his right hand. He did this at intervals coinciding with heightened passages in the chant, and each time he did this a cloud of coloured smoke rose from the lamp and drifted lazily into the dawn sky. The smoke was first red, then green, and then blue.

As the coloured smoke rose there came from Bork's men a strange sigh of wonder and astonishment.

The stones, it seemed, were demonstrating their awesome power.

Then Bork suspecting a trick, gave a harsh laugh, allowed a dreadful fury to fill his mind and soul, raised his much bloodied spear and prepared to lead his men into battle.

The time had come.

He Bork would show them that all this was just a harmless, empty, threat. He would show them that this menace could be easily destroyed.

And destroy them he would.

He would set an example and they would follow.

He swallowed his fear and faced his declared enemies.

CHAPTER 30

⸙ **DAWN** ⸙

*A*villa knew from the moment of his awaking that today, even the next few hours, would test his will, his courage, and above all his belief, to vindication or destruction, and that if he failed he would take this whole clan with him. He would also take their world back to the ancient ways. He felt alone and his heart was squeezed in fear, but with Sonlith's agreement he had set out his stall as the soothsayer had suggested and took hope from her prediction that Bork would die "of his own making, but not by his own hand." But puzzle as he might he could not fathom this riddle.

Before sunrise on this celebrated day of mid-summer, he had assembled the council members at the circle. The women and children had been moved well away, whilst a precious few men who possessed any kind of weapon were set to guard them.

Those at the centre saw the army move into position to stand fiercely round the edge of the outer bank, whilst two groups were arrayed just outside the entrance to the inner ring. The huge stones stood bedecked with flowers - unyielding - waiting it seemed for events to begin. Powerful forces were in the air and all present felt them and trembled.

The stones stood erect, impassive, dwarfing the humans who had stood them in this very place. Their invisible power was felt by both defenders and their uninvited foe.

When The Boar appeared a great shout rose from the army, and thrill of fear ran through the people of the sun, and they knew they were facing near certain death.

Sonlith and Avilla turned to face the enemy gathered to render their destruction and with a terrific struggle set their minds to the task of welcoming the dawning sun.

As the thin bright edge of the sun's orb appeared in the man-made gap in the trees on the horizon they began the sacred chant that would honour the power of the sun to bring forth abundant growth and a rich harvest.

The sun began its climb, and gathering their courage from each other, the council member's chant grew louder swelling to a long, deep and harmonious prayer of hope and promise. The power invested in the stones responded, increased and infected all present with ancient mystery, changing all who heard for ever.

The army knew its job, but bitterness, resentment and a graven fear of the stones and the power they held affected them and sapped their resolve. Most hated attacking unarmed men and feared terrible retribution from unknown invincible forces brought into being on this special day. Bork had ignored their protests and threatened any deserters with death. The cauldron of his hatred was about to boil over.

All present felt that the hand of destiny was about to define the future, and afterwards their lives and the lives of countless people to come would never be the same.

The future was on the very brink of being re-defined.

Slowly the priestly chant grew louder and the army gradually became hushed as blood red, the full disc of the sun filled the man made gap on the horizon where it seemed to pause as the priest's chant reached a crescendo and suddenly ceased, leaving a silence devoid of even the slightest sound. The world it seemed held its breath.

For Bork this was the very pinnacle of his striving, the army was ready and victory was in his grasp.

He stood in front of his troops with Drng nearby awaiting his signal to attack. He prepared his mind for the fight, allowing the acid bile of hate to fill his heart and mind.

This then was the moment for which his whole life had been a preparation. All the struggle, conflict and death was gathered into this single act.

Now............ Bork the Boar, raised his spear shoulder high to lead the assault -

- and with a great yell -

'CHARGE!' - He charged into the open space, hurling himself hatred driven towards the waiting pair with Avilla as his target - his revenge was within his grasp.

Avilla knew his own death was about to take place, and watched the charging animal that was Bork with fear knowing himself to be the target, he found that he was unable to move to defend himself.

His death had become a certainty.

Then amazingly, with the army fully ready to follow Bork into the fray - not a single man stirred. Bork's army stood still and silent, every eye on the charging figure.

Committed now, and unaware that he was alone, Bork ran on still roaring loudly, confident that the army would follow him.

Again, not a man in the army stirred, mesmerized by the hurtling, shouting figure of hate and fury that was The Boar. He moved with that strange rolling motion cause by his shorter leg, but he was still swift and speedily closed the gap to his quarry.

Suddenly, as if to an order, but none was given, three javelins arced into the sky from the ranks of the army. The first was the most accurate, and powered by gravity as it fell it entered Bork's un-armoured back, its sharpened blade passing between ribs and spine it entered his heart, its point even just appearing through his leather chest armour, spraying his life's blood in front of him. The second missed him and bedded itself harmlessly in the ground in front of him. The third shaft dropped short but lodged in his right calf causing him to crash forward to lie without life just a spear's length in front of the trembling Avilla. His last view of life was his own blood splashed on the grass now fully lit by the glory that was the risen sun.

And thus was the prophecy fulfilled, for he had been killed in a conflict of his own creation - but in the event by the hand of another.

There was a moment of complete silence followed by a great sigh as if the world had suddenly relaxed. Sonlith and Avilla waited fearfully for the army to move, but to their intense relief Drng plunged his spear point downwards into the soft earth to indicate his reluctance to fight, to be immediately followed by the men in the front rank, and then slowly by the rest.

The rays of the sun were now well above the stones, which seemed to reach up to meet it, whilst all present stood in respectful silence to watch the yellow orb rise into a pure blue sky, and all were bathed in its warmth. It even fell on Bork who lay where he had fallen in front of the stones, his red blood on the grass imitating the sun.

Slowly the army, subdued by these momentous events, gathered itself together and separately and in small groups retired quietly to their camp.

It was all over. Bork's drive to set his world back to the old ways and to become the first ruler of both North and South Realms of Kingdoms was finished.

The future was waiting.

The people gradually emerged to join the white clad members of the council and stood around excitedly discussing their escape from certain disaster. Bork's body lay unattended and ignored. Sonlith and Avilla simply stood speechlessly smiling, finding it difficult to believe their good fortune. Only Elln was joyously jumping with unsuppressed glee.

Stunned by the death of Bork and somewhat at a loss as to what to do next with no leader to order him and realising that he was now in sole command, it took Drng a little time to remember words whispered to him of Bork's wicked instructions to have Fellysin killed. When the realisation returned he felt his heart turn to ice and fear such as he had never before known gripped him. He schooled himself not to panic and set out to find her. And find her he did. She stood, ashen faced outside her tent. Her hands were tied in front of her and each of her arms was gripped by one of Bork's two grim faced bodyguard-henchmen.

No-one spoke or moved and slowly from nowhere curious people arrived and formed a silent circle around the small group.

Drng tried to think what to say to effect Fellysin's safe release, conscious of the fact that he now had no weapon whilst both guards were fully armed.

He had to act.

`I am now your commander. Release her immediately or suffer the consequences.' he ordered as authoratively as he knew.

But then, even before Drng could move to save Fellysin, a bronze knife flashed in the now bright sunlight.

Terck the body-guard it was who held the weapon high for a moment before plunging it downwards in a glinting arc.

The knife severed the rope holding Fellysin's wrists and she was free.

To cheers from the watchers she ran into Drng's waiting arms, whilst the guards Terck and Sollin melted away.

****

Some time later the delayed troops collected by Greth Avilla's adopted son arrived to find all at peace and both he and the men were truly glad that they would not be required to fight when they saw the sheer size of the Boar's army encamped nearby.

It was Avilla who was the first to realise that all spears were decorated so that each could be recognised by its owner, and so the owners of the three that were hurled at Bork could thus be identified. And this if it happened would lead to bitterness and recriminations. He decided it must not be allowed to happen. So whilst everyone's attention was elsewhere he and Elln collected the three javelins from where

Bork lay. He then instructed Elln to take them to the river and throw them in as far as he could downstream.

Elln was a bright lad and guessed the reason for Avilla's request and promptly did as he was bid. The weapons struck the water with a satisfying splash and promptly vanished beneath the grey rippling surface.

Later that day the Bork's body was collected by members of his army and by Drng's order buried with his spear and personal belongings but without scant ceremony some distance from the stone circle. The place was left unmarked.

It was many weeks later that Terck realised the significance of Lit pill's asking to borrow his spare javelin and then later claiming he had lost it. When his time came he took this knowledge with him to his ancestors having told not a living person.

Fellysin had noticed that Drng had set forth on that fateful day with his two intricately carved spears but returned with only one. This she never ever referred to.

Avilla observed that one of the weapons was lighter than the other two, such as a woman might own - and wondered.

Bork's killer thus went unpunished to everyone's relief.

****

Only the story singers would keep the memory of Bork the Boar, son of Tallon, and his failed quest alive - in song.

> `He marched with his army the length of this land,
> To die as foreseen.
> "Of his own making, but not his own hand."

It was to have been.'

Yorg

CHAPTER 31

❦ **AFTERWARDS** ❧

*O*nce the turmoil which followed the mid-summer's day events settled down, life at the great stone circle gradually returned to what it was before. There were no formal celebrations marking the end of the attempted military invasion, but there was a general air of thankfulness, even of joy about the place.

The first to move on were the story singers, and what a story the had to tell. They knew that people would find it hard to believe - but given time they would.

Drng in a powerful farewell speech dismissed the army and its followers and captured women. A few like Noon stayed, most left in small groups to find their way back to their original homes, but not before they had been given a walk around tour of the stone circle and its environment and had the 'new way' explained to them. Most became its ambassadors.

Fellysin stayed with Drng under Avilla's roof for some considerable time whilst Fellysin gave birth to a very healthy boy.

Elln was fascinated by Skill Drng's pet wolf with whom he made friends. Skill returned from a lone trip to the woods heavily pregnant and gave birth to two males which left to return to the wild, and a female which became tame and to which Elln gave the name Brand (meaning brave). The pair became inseparable.

Lit pill also stayed, for a while, and with Drng's help invented a harness for Drng's horse Flame so that it could help to move the stones into place and to pull a crude plough which Lit pill also created. This led to the capture and corralling of a small number of wild horses a couple of which, after many trials and mistakes, they were able to tame and put to work.

Greth's temporary army was also sent home, but not without grateful thanks from Sonlith, and the inevitable lecture tour. After which Greth was assigned to help to educate Elln with who he had become a close friend.

Sonlith continued to be head of the great circle community, which he was more than happy to do, although he never took a woman. He and Avilla agreed that Elln should succeed him when old enough - subject of course to be formally voted to that exalted position.

Bork's henchmen-bodyguards Terck and Sollin made their peace with Drng shortly after the debacle and then quietly vanished. Nothing more is known about them.

After some years Drng and Fellysin found that they were homesick for the scenery and people of the north and decided to return. Avilla had now fallen for the still very lovely Noon and the pair were joined in a ceremony in the stone circle conducted by Sonlith, and after the nuptial celebrations agreed to join Drng, Fellysin and their son on the trek north; Avilla being anxious to meet his natural son.

Keen to stay with those he trusted as friends Lit pill pleaded to join them, and to his tearful surprise found that they were overjoyed to have him do so, for he was much loved and respected. Sonlith would miss him. Avilla was delighted.

One spring after long and tearful farewells this small group complete with Drng's wolf and horse set out, and after a few easily overcome difficulties arrived at the small stone circle now completed by Herik who welcomed them happily. He feasted them right royally and they exchanged all the news.

The clan to which Bork had laid siege had joined Herik. Noon therefore was re-united with friends and family, one of whom Herik had chosen to be his woman. They now had several children and the clan was contented and prosperous.

They eventually said goodbye to Herik and continued north. Noon said goodbye to her clan and stayed with Avilla.

They found Tallon's old clan barely surviving. Noon easily took to Avilla's natural son. Then over just a few happy years this small group of friends turned the fortunes of the clan around. And with their knowledge gained from Sonlith and company the clan created a much visited example of the rich new way of life. Lit pill's intellect and inventive spirit played a major part in the clan's recovery but not without many an hilarious episode - he was much loved and eventually settled down with a very understanding lady; she needed to be.

The story singers still visited and the friends were never tired of hearing of their exploits in song.

****

In time the great stone circle gets completed. But growing river communication and trade pressures become more important, and the great circle gets left behind as the centre of the Southern Realm.

Travel becomes very much easier, trade increases, and the North and the South Realms begin to merge, and clans no longer isolated begin to form a loosely defined nation, and fledgling agriculture begins to change the landscape.

Bork's world vanished with him.

A new sense of optimism for the future prevailed spread no doubt, with the help of the story singers.

A brand-new future had begun.

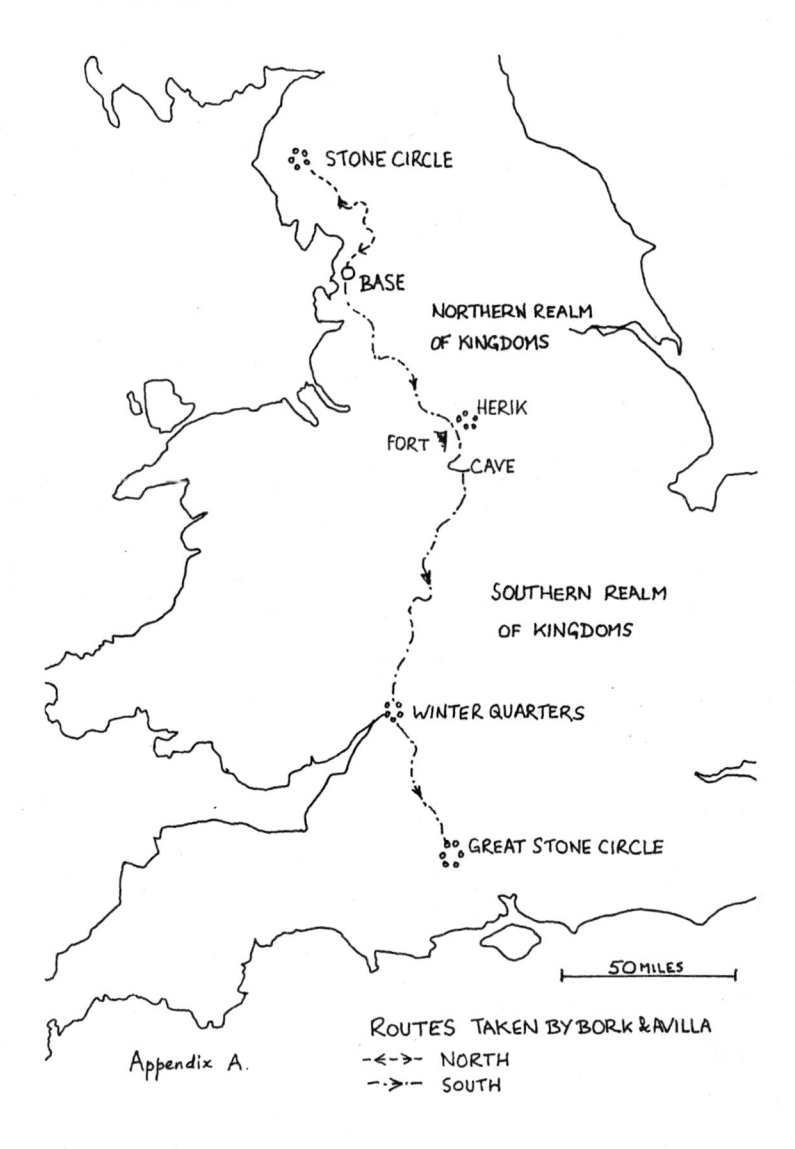

APPENDIX A

Appendix A.

Routes taken by Bork & Avilla
- -<->- NORTH
- -·>·- SOUTH

APPENDIX B

THE ROUTE & TIMETABLE OF MAIN EVENTS

YEAR 1.—

SPRING Avilla kills Tallon @ base

SUMMER
           Bork takes command
AUTUMN

WINTER Bork Prepares to go North

YEAR 2. —

SPRING Bork goes North &   1st Clan offers help
        then farther North   1st Stone circle/fight

SUMMER Returns to base

AUTUMN Avilla goes South & visits Herick's clan

WINTER Avilla hides in cave with story singers

BORK and the stones of power

YEAR 3.—

SPRING	Bork marches on South -	Avilla continues on South -	
SUMMER	following Avilla	ahead of Bork	Bork reaches Herik
AUTUMN	Bork arrives at big river	Avilla arrives at big stone circle	Sonlith's clan welcomes Avilla
WINTER	Bork's winter camp at big river		

YEAR 4. —

SPRING	Bork continues on South	Avilla joins Sonlith	Sonlith's clan prepares for war
SUMMER	Arrives at big Stone Circle	------Battle----------	

APPENDIX C

LIST OF MAIN CHARACTERS

Tallon	Clan chief at the beginning
Zapallor	Tallon's soothsayer
Avilla	Tallon's younger brother
Bork	Tallon's son and heir
Chine	Tallon's woman and Bork's mother
Terck & Sollin	Tallon's/Bork's henchmen-bodyguards
Yorg & Pladge	Story Singers
Drng	Soldier and Bork's second in command
Fellysin	Beauty and Drng's love
Lit Pill	Accident prone - joins Bork
Flame	Drng's / Bork's horse
Skill	Drng's tame wolf
Walther	Story singer
Jedd	Story singer
Greth	Story singer & Avilla's adopted son
Herik	Clan chief (white stone district)
Noon	Woman captured by Bork
Joonry & Hapt	Story singers
Sonlith	Chief of Great Stone Circle clan
Pallin	Sonlith's deputy
Elln	Sonlith's sister's son
Bron	Avilla's natural son

ISBN 142516894-9